GHOSTLY DECEITS

A Harper Harlow Mystery Book Three

LILY HARPER HART

HarperHart Publications

ONE

"If this was the zombie apocalypse I would shoot you in the leg and leave you behind so I could make my getaway."

Harper Harlow rolled her eyes and tried to ignore her best friend Zander Pritchett's words as she crouched behind a large tombstone and cocked her head to the side, listening as she tried to get a feeling for where Archibald Bingham Nedstrom – with a name like that, of course he would be a pain – hid.

"Did you hear me, Harper?" Zander hissed, lowering himself so he was at eye-level with Harper. "I would shoot you in the leg and let the zombies eat you so I could escape. That's how angry I am with you."

Harper loved Zander dearly – including his dramatic fits – but there were times she wanted to feed him to the zombies, too. This would be one of them. Thankfully the lifelong friends were not mired in a zombie apocalypse. No, flesh-eating mutants weren't coming to eat their brains. Instead Harper and Zander – co-owners of Ghost Hunters, Inc. – were trying to capture a ticked off ghost.

"I heard you, Zander," Harper replied, her tone clipped. "You would shoot me and leave me for dead. However, I want you to know that I would survive the gunshot, outsmart the zombies, and sneak into your house when you were sleeping later that night so I could replace all of your Egyptian cotton sheets with polyester blends."

Zander's mouth dropped open as the potential horror washed over him. "That's the meanest thing you've ever said to me."

"How is that meaner than saying you want me to be eaten by zombies?" Harper asked, frustrated.

"You know I break out if I have cheap sheets," Zander said.

"Whatever," Harper muttered, jolting when she heard someone moaning over her left shoulder. She risked a glance and found the spot empty, although something was close ... and she had a feeling it was Archibald. "I think he's trying to draw us away from the tombstone and out into the open."

"Well, we're not doing that," Zander said, resting his back against the ornate tombstone in question and making a face. "I'm not doing anything a ghost wants me to do. I know we're supposed to be helping spirits move to the other side because it's a good thing, but this ghost is a douche."

Harper pursed her lips to keep from laughing. Zander was the only person she knew who would opt to run a ghost hunting business and yet hate ghosts. There was something almost ... poetic ... about his dislike of the spiritually displaced. "He's not a douche," she corrected. "He's ... ."

A potted plant from two graves over flew through the air and crashed against the tombstone Harper and Zander hid behind. Zander saw it a split-second before Harper lost her head and yanked her closer to the ground to protect her.

"You were saying?" Zander asked dryly.

Harper made a face. "He might be a douche."

"And I *might* be interested in men instead of women," Zander countered. "Come on! Admit he's a douche."

"I think it's because he has such a horrible name," Harper said, refusing to bow to Zander's demands. "You would be unhappy if you had that name, too."

"You have a point," Zander said. "That's still no reason to take it out on us. We didn't kill him. We aren't responsible for his douche-y soul still hanging around. We're definitely not responsible for him throwing that plant at us."

Harper sighed, resigned. "Fine, Zander. He's a douche. That doesn't change the fact that we've been hired for a job. We have to put him to rest. Whether he's a douche or not has absolutely no bearing on what we're doing."

Zander crossed his arms over his chest and narrowed his eyes. "You just don't want to admit that I'm right. That's what this is all about. You've never been able to accept the fact that I'm smarter than you."

"You are not smarter than me," Harper shot back. "We took IQ tests in college. Do you remember that? What did they say?"

"We got the exact same score," Zander answered.

"So how are you smarter than me?" Harper challenged.

"I have street smarts," Zander replied, tapping his temple for emphasis. "We're both book smart. On the street, though, you would be the first one plugged in a gang shooting. That's all I'm saying. It's not anything bad, but it is the way of the world we live in."

Harper wrinkled her nose. "In what world is that not anything bad?"

"My world," Zander answered, snapping his fingers in Harper's face for emphasis. "Now you need to focus on the problem at hand. Archibald is a douche. We're in a cemetery after dark – and I told you I would never do that so I still can't figure out how you convinced me it was a good idea. We've been hired to put his soul to rest and we're supposed to be home by nine because Jared is grilling steaks."

Harper smiled at the mention of her boyfriend Jared Monroe. They'd only been dating for a few weeks, but even the idea of seeing him was still thrilling. He was a police officer who accepted her ghost hunting ways. In her mind he was practically perfect. It didn't hurt that he was smoking hot either.

"Oh, wipe that goofy grin off your face," Zander chided. "You get all moony whenever his name comes up – like you're in a PG romance novel, which is funny because you get horny whenever you see him in person, like you're in a porn movie. Now, I'm not begrudging you a nice roll in the hay. Lord knows you deserve it given your life of loneliness before Jared, but now is not the time to lose your head in his dreamy eyes."

"I wish you would stop calling Jared's eyes 'dreamy'," Harper said. "It freaks him out."

"They *are* dreamy."

"I know, but he's still getting used to the fact that you climb into bed with us some mornings to tell me about your date the previous evening," Harper said. "He's having trouble adjusting to our lack of inhibitions."

"Why should we have inhibitions?" Zander challenged, lifting his head when he heard Archibald moan and throw something against the nearby mausoleum. "Knock it off! We're having an important discussion. Stop being a douche for five minutes and then we'll get to you. Sheesh!"

"I think it's odd for Jared because another guy is sharing a bed with both of us," Harper said, choosing her words carefully. "He's really worried we're going to be naked when you try it one morning."

"You lock the door when you're naked," Zander countered. "I know because I've tried going in several other mornings. That's how you missed the story when I broke up with Adam because he had mushrooms growing between his toes."

"He didn't have actual mushrooms," Harper argued. Zander always found a reason to fall in love – and then he found another reason ten seconds later to fall out of love. The reasons were getting more and more dramatic. "He had Athlete's Foot. That's not the same thing as growing mushrooms between your toes."

"Athlete's Foot is a fungal infection," Zander said.

"I know."

"What are mushrooms?"

"They're technically a fungus," Harper said, seeing where Zander was going with the comparison. "It's still not the same thing."

"It's gross," Zander said.

"You have issues."

"We're not talking about my issues right now," Zander said. "We're talking about Jared's issues. Are you saying I can't visit you on mornings when he sleeps over because he's homophobic?"

Harper knit her eyebrows together. "I'm pretty sure that's not even remotely what I said." She caught a hint of movement out of the corner of her eye and shifted so she could watch Archibald float closer. He seemed interested in them and yet angered by their presence at the same time.

"No. You said Jared doesn't like it when I get in bed with you and gossip because he doesn't want me to see him naked. Like I would jump him or something because my hormones are out of control and I'm a deviant. I get it."

Harper recognized the obstinate tilt of Zander's chin and inwardly groaned. Not only was she never going to hear the end of this, but now he was going to take a passive aggressive approach with Jared until things exploded into a screaming match. That had "nightmare" written all over it.

"That's not it," Harper argued. "He's just terrified you're going to come in when we're ... you know ... doing it."

This time it was Zander's turn to make a face. "Seriously? If you're having sex, you should be able to talk about it."

"Don't take that tone with me," Harper warned. "It's not my fault you keep making jokes about 'morning wood' as you're climbing under the covers. Jared likes you. He's just ... uncomfortable ... sharing a bed with you."

"I see how it is," Zander said, his tone shifting in pitch. "We've been best friends since we were five and now that you've got a boyfriend who can't deal with the utter fabulous nature of my being, I'm the odd man out. I get it."

"That's not it," Harper said, hating how whiny she sounded. "You know I love you more than anything in this world. You're the best friend I've ever had. I don't have a problem with you crawling into bed with us so you can tell me about your date.

"You just need to stop talking about him waxing his chest, changing from flannel to silk boxers, and generally commenting on the size of his nipples," she said.

"I'm sorry, but they're freaky nipples," Zander said. "If I was dating Jared we'd have to get them shaved down or something. I think they're big."

"They're nipples, Zander," Harper snapped. "They look like normal nipples."

"They're bigger than mine."

"Have you ever considered that your nipples are freakishly small?"

"Of course not," Zander scoffed. "We both know I could be a nipple model."

"There's no such thing as a nipple model."

"I'll bet you twenty bucks nipple models exist," Zander challenged. "I'm going to look it up when we get home."

"I can't wait."

"And when I do, I'm going to take photos of my nipples and Jared's nipples and send them to a talent agent so he can judge which ones are better," Zander added.

"I can't wait to see how you explain why you're taking photos of Jared's nipples to him," Harper said. "That's not going to make him feel uncomfortable at all. Have you considered that things like this are exactly why he's weirded out when you hop into bed with us?"

"You're my best friend," Zander countered. "It's not weird to gossip in bed with your best friend. Would he have a problem if another woman climbed into bed with you?"

"Probably not," Harper conceded. "I think that's every straight man's favorite fantasy. I would have a problem if Jared's female best friend hopped into bed with us, though."

Zander arched a challenging eyebrow. "Even if she was gay?"

"Even if," Harper confirmed. "It's weird. I want Jared focused on me when we're in bed together. I can see why it bothers Jared for me to focus on you when I'm in bed with him. Are you honestly saying you wouldn't have a problem if the guy you were dating brought a third guy into bed?"

Zander's features took on a whimsical look. "That sounds like the perfect Saturday night."

Harper made a face that would've been comical under different circumstances. "You say that because you think it makes you sound cool, but we both know that would be the worst night of your life. Can you imagine the faults you would find with two men to focus on?

"Think of all the unevenly trimmed toenails," she continued.

"Think of the rampant nose hair. That's double the chance for briefs. That's double the chance for butt hair. Heck, that's double the chance for pit stains."

"You really know how to take the joy out of a fantasy," Zander groused, although his expression softened. "I kind of get what you're saying about Jared. I didn't think it was a big deal when I crawled into bed with you guys because I don't see female parts when I look at you. I just see my best friend Harper. You don't have female parts as far as I'm concerned.

"From his perspective he sees a romantic rival with better muscles and abs," he continued. "It has to be torture for him."

Harper bit her lip to keep from laughing. Of course Zander would take her comments that way. "I ... that probably is what he's worried about. I'm sure he doesn't want to admit it, though, so you might not want to bring it up when you see him."

"Of course not," Zander said, waving Harper's concerns away. "I don't want to upset him or make him feel inferior due to my godlike ways. I understand. From now on, I'll only crawl into bed with you when you're alone."

"I'm sure that will make him feel better," Harper said, grinning at the thought. "Speaking of Jared, though, I'm hungry. We should get this show on the road."

"We definitely should do that," Zander agreed. "Where did Archie the Douche go?"

Harper pointed to Archibald's serene spirit as he floated a few feet away, seemingly engrossed in their conversation. "I think he's calmer now. He's floating right there and watching us. He probably saw the way we interacted and the love we have for one another and remembered his life before it was so tragic."

"Yeah, that sounds exactly like what happened," Zander said, sarcasm practically dripping from his tongue. "Did our friendship touch you, Archibald? Is that why you're listening?" He couldn't see ghosts, but he believed Harper when she told him Archibald was close.

"No." Archibald shook his ethereal head.

"What did he say?" Zander asked.

Harper ignored the question. "What calmed you down?" she asked, genuinely curious.

"I've now officially seen everything," Archibald answered, making a face. "You two are sick, by the way."

"We're here to help you," Harper argued. "There's a better place for you out there if you let go of this life and the hate keeping you here."

"Hate isn't keeping me here," Archibald argued.

"What's keeping you here?"

"I get my jollies in weird ways – like your friend here," Archibald replied, inclining his chin in Zander's direction. "Well, not exactly the same way. I still like a good fight, though."

"Are you ready to move on?" Harper asked hopefully. "Do you want to see what's waiting for you when you crossover?"

Archibald tilted his head to the side, the mausoleum visible through his filmy countenance. "I'm good."

Harper stilled, surprised. "You're good?"

"I don't want to leave," Archibald said. "I'm happy here."

"But you're alone," Harper prodded. "Don't you want to move on and be with your loved ones?"

"They were royal jackasses for the most part, so I'm good," Archibald said. "In this place I get to nap when I want, scare people whenever the mood strikes, and occasionally see people do the dirty because there's some sort of cemetery club that's supposed to be like the Mile High Club. Why would I want to leave that?"

Harper was floored. "But … people really sneak in and have sex on graves? That's so gross."

"Is that what he said? That's really gross," Zander intoned. "Only freaks would do that."

"Says the guy who wants to take photos of another guy's nipples," Archibald deadpanned. "It doesn't matter, though. I'm not leaving and you can't make me."

Harper planted her hands on her narrow hips. "Archibald, I'm afraid that's simply not true," she said. "You can't stay here. The cemetery managers say you're terrorizing people. That girl you goosed the other day was only seventeen."

"And she had a nice, firm butt," Archibald said, grinning at the memory. "I really liked her."

"And yet she was still not legally an adult."

"She was close enough," Archibald said. "If you're old enough to need a bra and not wear one, I think that's plenty old for me."

"You're a pig," Harper snapped. "You need to let go and embrace your hereafter. You're stagnating here."

"I'm fine with that," Archibald said.

"But ... ." Harper was at a loss for words. "There's a better place out there."

"We're not all looking for better places," Archibald said, floating around Zander and moving behind Harper so he could study her more closely. "Some of us are happy with our lot in life. I'm one of the happy people. You can take your platitudes and promises and look somewhere else for someone to help. I'm happy here, and there's nothing you can do about it."

Archibald pinched Harper's rear end and caused her to squeal as she swiveled.

"Hey!"

"See, that was fun," Archibald said, his face splitting with a wide smile.

"What happened?" Zander asked, blindly letting his gaze bounce across the cemetery.

"Listen, pervert, you're passing over whether you like it or not," Harper said, scowling. "I don't care if you want to stay. You're going."

Archibald didn't look particularly worried. "Do you really think you can force me?"

"I really do."

"Well, bring it on," Archibald said. "I love it when war is afoot."

TWO

J ared Monroe checked the marinating steaks before turning to the Brussels sprouts and dousing them with olive oil and salt and pepper. He tossed them in a bag so he could shake the ingredients and then poured the contents onto a cookie sheet. He glanced at the clock, frowning when he realized how late it was getting. Harper and Zander were supposed to be home by now. He hoped something wasn't wrong.

If someone would've told Jared three months ago that he would be absolutely besotted with a feisty blonde who happened to hunt ghosts for a living, he would've called them crazy (and probably a few more things that were just as colorful). He definitely wouldn't have believed them. Here he was, though, cooking dinner for Harper and Zander while they did … well, he honestly had no idea what they did when they were out on a job. He'd been meaning to talk to Harper about that because he was dying to tag along on an outing. She seemed embarrassed at the prospect, but he was genuinely curious.

Before Harper came into his life, Jared didn't believe in the supernatural. He thought it was hokey superstition and nothing more. Now he truly believed Harper was gifted and could talk to ghosts. He still grappled with what that would mean for their future, but he was determined they would have a future so he knew he would find a way to deal with it.

The sound of a car door slamming in the front of the house caught Jared's attention and he moved in that direction. He opened the front door, an admonishment for being late on his tongue, and then burst out laughing when he caught sight of Harper and Zander.

The willowy blonde was caked with mud, her hair matted and almost completely covered. Zander was even worse off because he appeared to have rolled around in leaves and other debris after being coated with the mud. If he didn't know better, he would think they were dressed for Halloween. Jared wasn't familiar with all of Zander's quirks, but he knew the man didn't like getting dirty. This definitely wasn't on purpose.

"What happened?" Jared asked, fighting to rein in his laughter.

"Archibald was a douche," Zander said, trudging up the front walkway. "He was the world's biggest douche."

"I see," Jared said, pressing his lips together as he focused on Harper. She was lovely on a normal day, tall for a woman and slim. She didn't wear a lot of makeup and was naturally pretty. That was one of the things he loved most about her. "How did you like Archibald?"

"Zander is right," Harper said, scratching the side of her nose with a filthy finger. "Archibald was a douche."

"Did you get rid of him?"

"Yes, and it was a lovely send off," Zander deadpanned. "Harper kept arguing that he wasn't really a bad guy and he only remained behind because he was disgruntled with life due to his unfortunate name. Then Archibald explained he didn't want to leave because he enjoyed scaring people and occasionally watching couples do the dirty in the cemetery."

"That's gross," Jared said, reaching to brush Harper's hair away from her face and then thinking better of it. Zander wasn't the only one with an aversion to getting dirty. "So what happened?"

"Do you mean before Archibald started throwing mud at us or after he pinched my butt and declared it okay for an old woman?" Harper asked.

Jared tried to hold in his laughter, but failed. "Oh, Heart ... ."

Harper made a face. "It's not funny."

"It's a little funny," Jared said.

"It's really not," Zander said. "It's been a terrible day. All I want to do now is to take a shower and have you feed me."

"The food is ready to cook," Jared said. "I think you both need showers first."

"I definitely need a shower," Harper agreed, moving to kiss Jared's cheek by way of greeting and frowning when he pulled away. "Seriously? You're not going to kiss me after the horrible day I've had?"

"I'm going to kiss you senseless once you shower and change your clothes."

"I think that's kind of offensive," Harper said. "If you truly cared, you would want to kiss me no matter what."

"I think you're playing games because you want to manipulate me," Jared countered. "I'm going to cut that little maneuver off at the pass. While you and Zander get cleaned up, I will handle dinner. After that, I will massage you for an entire hour while you drink red wine and tell me about your day."

Harper's face split with a wide smile. "You had me at massage."

"I know I did," Jared said, smirking.

"What about me?" Zander whined. "I had just as terrible a day as Harper did."

"I'm not massaging you."

Zander scowled.

"I did, however, buy you a blueberry cheesecake from that deli you like downtown," Jared said. "I think it's called Whisper Cove Delicacies. Harper said it was your favorite."

"You had me at cheesecake," Zander said, taking Jared by surprise when he planted a firm kiss on his cheek. "I love coming home to find the little woman has prepared dinner for us."

Jared narrowed his eyes. He found Zander's sense of humor endearing most of the time. On the occasions it missed, though, he wanted to throttle him. "I'm going to spit in your food if you're not careful."

"You wouldn't dare."

"I'm going to put mushrooms on your steak," Jared threatened.

"Since you're not over that guy growing mushrooms between his toes, I think it's going to ruin your dinner if I do it."

"Fine," Zander said, rolling his eyes. "You win."

"Thank you," Jared said, giving Zander and Harper a wide berth as they walked into the house. He couldn't help but chuckle as he heard them chat during their walk to the bedrooms.

"He's really bossy and mean sometimes," Zander lamented.

"I think he's cute," Harper said.

"He does have dreamy eyes," Zander agreed.

"Don't go there."

"You don't go there," Zander countered, poking Harper's side. "I still maintain I would be the better nipple model. I don't care what you say."

"In your dreams."

Jared had no idea what they were talking about, but he left them to their idle gossip and cleanup and returned to cooking. Despite Zander's teasing tone, Jared found he really didn't mind cooking for the dynamic duo. He had no idea how it happened, but he was suddenly domesticated.

"That's an interesting development," he muttered to himself, rolling the idea through his busy mind. He didn't give it much thought before returning to his Brussels sprouts. He was definitely domesticated, but he was also happy.

He could live with that.

"SO HOW DID YOU GUYS FINALLY CATCH THE DOUCHE-Y wonder?" Jared asked two hours later, kneading his fingers into Harper's sore muscles as she sat between his legs on the living room floor.

"Harper tricked him into chasing her by threatening to make sure the only butts coming to the cemetery would be old ones and I dropped the dreamcatcher in front of him when he wasn't looking and we absorbed him right there," Zander explained, wearily relaxing on the couch. "That cheesecake was amazing, man. I definitely needed that after my crappy day."

"Everything was amazing," Harper said, a low moan escaping as

Jared hit a particularly sensitive spot. The moans were doing something to him. He couldn't lie – not even to himself. He also wasn't going to follow his inner caveman and toss Harper over his shoulder and carry her into the bedroom. He promised her an hour-long massage and that's what she was going to get.

"I grilled steaks, bought a cheesecake, and roasted Brussels sprouts," Jared said, feigning modesty. "It's not like a cured cancer."

"It was close enough," Zander said. "I'm so stuffed I could pass out right here."

"Me, too," Harper said.

"Oh, you can't do that, Harp," Zander chided. "Jared doesn't like it when we sleep together so you have to go to your own bedroom."

Jared stilled, cocking an eyebrow as his gaze bounced between Harper and Zander. "What?"

"It's nothing," Harper said hurriedly, straightening her back and gesturing to her shoulders. "Rub, please."

"I'll continue to rub you when you tell me what's going on."

Harper sighed. "I *might* have told Zander how it makes you uncomfortable when he climbs into bed with us some mornings."

Jared ran his tongue over his teeth as he considered how to answer. It did drive him crazy when Zander ended up in bed with them, but not for the reasons Harper and Zander thought. "I … ."

"Don't worry about it, man," Zander interrupted, holding his hand up. "I understand. Harper explained about you being insecure because I'm so much hotter than you and have better muscles. I thought it might be because you were embarrassed I have better nipples, too, but Harper says that's not the case. I promise to only climb in bed with Harper when you're not here."

"Well, since I plan on spending every night possible with Harper, that's not going to leave you a lot of options," Jared said. "I honestly don't have a problem with you and Harper gossiping in bed because you're hot. Although … what's wrong with my nipples?" Jared pulled his shirt out and looked inside. He'd never given his nipples much thought, but now that's all he could focus on.

"There's nothing wrong with your nipples," Harper said. "Zander doesn't like them because they're bigger than his."

"That's not the only thing that's bigger," Jared muttered, causing Harper to snicker and Zander to scowl.

"Do you want to measure?" Zander challenged.

"We're not in high school," Jared replied.

"I think you're worried you'll lose."

Jared worried Zander was right so he decided to change the subject. "I have no problem with you two gossiping in bed," he said. "I have a problem with you not knocking before you come into the bedroom, Zander ... and there's nothing wrong with my nipples."

"I happen to love your nipples, honey," Harper cooed. "Now rub my back."

Jared sighed but did as instructed.

Zander mulled over Jared's statement. "I can knock," he said after a few moments. "I think that's fair. I honestly didn't realize I wasn't knocking. Harper and I generally have an open door policy on bedrooms. I get it, though. I promise to knock from here on out."

"That's great," Jared said. "I appreciate it."

"You still have freakishly big nipples," Zander said.

Jared rolled his eyes. "Speaking of nipples ... wait, that's not a proper transition. I need to get away from the nipple talk, though, so I'm going to change the subject to something completely different."

"I'm game," Zander said. "Let's talk about how old Harper's butt feels."

"I will kill you," Harper hissed, reaching over to pinch the inside of Zander's ankle.

"Ow!"

"Your butt is beautiful, Heart," Jared said, smirking as he watched Zander glare at Harper. "I happen to think it's one of your best features."

"Thank you." Harper's response was prim and pleased.

"He's just saying that because he wants to get lucky later," Zander supplied.

"I'm definitely going to kill you," Harper muttered.

"Can we focus on me a second?" Jared prodded. "I got a call from my old college buddy Josh Stoker and he invited me to one of those murder mystery events. His family owns a house on Harsens Island and it's supposed to be a big shindig and last several days."

"Are you going?" Harper asked.

"I already got the time off from work," Jared replied. "Mel said it's not a problem because things have been quiet. I haven't seen Josh since graduation and Harsens Island is only a half-hour away. I thought it would be fun."

"When is it?"

"I have to leave tomorrow," Jared answered.

"Oh." Harper's voice was laced with disappointment. "Are you going to be gone the whole week?"

"It's a weeklong event," Jared said. "It's some charity thing to raise money for children's cancer, but Josh wants me to come so we can catch up."

"That sounds … fun." Harper swallowed hard.

"Oh, don't worry, Harp. I'll be here to keep you company," Zander said. "We can gossip in bed as much as we want."

"I … sure," Harper said. "That sounds fun."

Jared considered stringing Harper along a little longer but opted against it. "The invitation is for two," he explained. "I was kind of hoping you would want to come with me."

Harper's eyes widened as she shifted to glance at Jared over her shoulder. "Really?" She looked so hopeful Jared couldn't stop his heart from rolling.

"Really," Jared confirmed, hauling her back so he could kiss her cheek. "Do you really think I want to be separated from you again after our last debacle?" He referenced a recent event that almost derailed the couple's relationship. His mother injured herself and needed help so Jared had to leave town for an extended trip. Jared was embarrassed to call Harper during their time apart because he didn't want to appear needy, so he left things hanging for ten days. It didn't go over well, and he practically had to beg her to forgive him when he returned. "Do you want to go to a murder mystery event with me?"

"I don't know," Harper hedged. "What would we have to do?"

"We would eat dinner and sleep in a fancy room," Jared replied. "We're supposed to participate in the mystery event, but it's not necessary if you don't want to do it. It's an island, so we can swim. They have a pool if you don't like the lake. There's also a tennis court. The food is supposed to be to die for. No pun intended."

"That sounds great, Harper," Zander said. "You have absolutely nothing to wear to those big dinners, though. We're going to have to shop all day tomorrow to get you ready."

"But ... ." Harper broke off, biting her lip.

"What's wrong?" Jared asked, pushing her hair away from her face. "If you don't want to go, we don't have to go. I can go out on my own for an afternoon to catch up with Josh. It won't be a big deal."

"I want to go," Harper said. "I just ... I'm not sure if I can leave GHI on such short notice. I am technically the boss."

"I didn't think of that," Jared said, his heart dropping. He'd been looking forward to time alone with Harper. He didn't even pause to consider the ramifications of her work situation.

"You're going," Zander said, taking Harper and Jared by surprise. "I'm also the boss at GHI. If we get a gig that requires your special talents, Harsens Island is a half-hour away. I can pick you up, take you to the job, and drop you back off. It will probably be a dead week anyway. I'm sure it will be fine."

"Dead week," Jared snickered.

"I thought you said we weren't in high school?" Zander challenged, causing Jared to sober.

"I want you to come with me," Jared said, digging his fingers into Harper's neck to remind her of what she would be missing if she declined the invitation. "Please."

"Okay," Harper said. "It sounds fun."

"It's definitely going to be fun," Zander said, causing Jared to grin as he reached for a pad of paper. "We need to make a list of the things we need to shop for tomorrow."

"Do we really have to shop?" Harper wasn't thrilled with the suggestion.

"You need dresses that don't make you look Amish and lingerie that doesn't make you look sexless," Zander shot back.

Harper turned her pleading eyes to Jared. "Can't you help me?"

"Oh, Heart, he had me at lingerie," Jared teased.

THREE

"Wow! You guys look as if you bought out the entire mall," Jared said the next evening, walking into Harper's bedroom with a garment bag draped across his arm and a small leather bag in the opposite hand. He hung the garment bag up in Harper's closet and moved to the pile of clothing on the bed. "How much did you spend?"

"A lot," Harper intoned, rubbing the spot between her eyebrows. "Zander said I needed options."

"Oh, my poor Harper," Jared said, offering her a soft kiss and lingering hug. He knew she hated shopping. "I missed you today."

"I missed you, too."

"And everyone missed me," Zander said, striding into the room. "Okay, it's time to show Jared what you bought and then pack."

"I can pack myself," Harper argued.

"No, you can't," Zander countered. "If I leave you to pack you'll fill your suitcase with jeans and T-shirts. That's not happening on my watch."

Jared sat down on the edge of the mattress to watch as Zander started sifting through the clothes. "This is kind of exciting. I can't believe I just said that, but there it is."

Harper scowled. "This is a conspiracy. I dress fine."

"You dress like you're trying to hide flaws and you don't have any flaws," Zander said. "Ask Jared. He looks at your body when you're naked all of the time. Do you think he wants to see you covered in a potato sack or showing off some skin?"

"This is the worst day ever," Harper muttered.

"Come here," Jared said, grabbing Harper around the waist and pulling her to his lap. "I think you look beautiful in whatever you want to wear. If this isn't your thing, you can wear whatever you want."

Zander tossed a tiny nightie – it happened to be blue and sheer – at Jared's head. "That's only one of the naughty things we bought."

Jared studied the item in question and smiled. "On the other hand, maybe you should listen to Zander."

"You're a pig," Harper said, her cheeks coloring as she grabbed the nightie from Jared.

"I can't wait to see you in that," Jared said, nuzzling her cheek. "If that makes me a pig ... well ... oink."

Zander laughed. "That was a very good response. So, we picked out several cocktail dresses and a few more simple spring dresses." Zander started holding them up so Jared could see them. "Harper insisted on a lot of black because she's afraid of too much color. I did the best I could on that front."

"I like that black one with the missing back," Jared said. "Definitely pack that one."

"I will," Zander said. "You should see the heels that go with it."

"I'm not wearing heels," Harper said.

"Oh, you're wearing them." Zander returned to the pile of clothes. "What's the deal with the dinner parties? I'm assuming she'll get away with simple dresses most nights."

"Yeah. Josh said only the first night and the last night were formal occasions," Jared said. "I brought a black suit."

"Men are lucky because they can wear one thing and look gorgeous," Harper said. "I have to dress up like a ... beauty queen ... and let you parade me around."

"I think you already look like a beauty queen," Jared said. "I am looking forward to seeing you in these dresses, though. Don't get me wrong or anything, because I love it when you dress down and don't make a fuss, but it's going to be fun to see you dressed up."

"I'm not sure it's going to be as fun as you seem to think it is," Harper argued.

"I think you're being a baby and you need to get over it," Zander chided. "Stop being a complete and total pain in the ass, Harp. This is a big deal for you. You're going away with your boyfriend for the first time. You're going to meet his college friend. That's a big deal."

"I know," Harper said, rubbing her stomach. "Trust me. I know."

"Are you nervous about that?" Jared asked, realization dawning. "Do you think you're not going to fit in or something?"

Harper shifted so she was facing Jared. "I have some concerns," she admitted. "What are we going to tell people that I do for a living?"

Jared was puzzled "Is there a reason we can't tell them the truth?"

"I hunt ghosts for a living."

"I know," Jared said. "I've been aware of it for quite some time now."

"But ... isn't your friend going to make fun of you for dating me?" Harper asked, worry flitting across her pleasing features.

Jared stilled, surprised. "Probably not," he said. "He's an open-minded guy. Even if he did, though, I don't care about that."

"You don't?" Harper wasn't convinced. "You don't care that we're going to a ritzy party and you're going to introduce one of your oldest friends to the ghost hunter you're dating?"

"No."

"Harp, do you want Jared to keep that to himself for now?" Zander asked, his face unreadable as he studied his best friend. Jared had no idea where he was going with the question, but he decided to let Zander handle the panic attack. He was good under pressure, and no one knew Harper better than he did.

"I honestly don't know," Harper admitted. "I feel ... exposed. I don't understand why. I'm usually fine with people knowing what I do for a living. I've never had this problem before. You know that."

"I *do* know that," Zander agreed. "Do you want to know what I think?"

"I'm not sure."

"I want to know what you think," Jared said, linking his fingers with Harper's and resting them on her stomach.

"I think you haven't liked anyone as much as you like Jared in … well … forever," Zander said. "Don't let that go to your head, Jared."

"Of course not," Jared replied dryly.

"You're still confident in who you are, but you're also worried that something will happen to make Jared change his mind about you," Zander said. "Personally, I don't think what a college friend thinks about you is going to matter. We'll ignore that for now."

"No, we're not going to ignore that," Jared interjected. "I don't care what anyone thinks about you but me, and I happen to like you just the way you are. I don't want you to change. Even more than that, though, I don't want you to think you have to change."

"That was a very sweet sentiment," Zander said. "I'm talking, though."

Jared shot Zander a dark look. "You're starting to get on my nerves."

Zander pressed his finger to his lips. "Shh."

Despite her nervous reaction, Harper couldn't help but giggle at Zander's antics. "Don't fight."

"We're not fighting," Zander said. "If we were fighting, I would be winning, though. Now, you're nervous about meeting an old friend of Jared's, but you're equally nervous about dressing up and playing nice with people you don't know.

"You're a business woman, Harp," he continued. "You know how to schmooze people. You're going to be fine. You know how to do small talk and you're going to have your hunky boyfriend at your side to make sure you're never uncomfortable."

"I'm not sure I like being called 'hunky.'"

"Shut up, Jared," Zander warned, never moving his eyes from Harper. "This is a big deal for you, Harp, and if you don't want the added pressure of explaining what you do for a living – which I totally understand, by the way – I have a suggestion for a lie that's not really a lie."

Harper leaned forward, intrigued. "What?"

"No, I don't want her to lie," Jared interjected. "There's no reason to lie. If people don't like what she does they can shove it up their ... ."

"It's quiet time, Jared," Zander said, patting his knee. "Let me handle this. I know what I'm doing."

"I want to hear his suggestion," Harper said. "I am really nervous. This might make me feel better."

"Fine." Jared gave in, resigned. "What is this grand idea?"

"You can tell people you give haunted Michigan tours," Zander suggested. "It's not a lie. We do them several times a year. It's part of our job. That will make you sound bohemian and chic and still allow you to keep the other part of our job – the one where you can see and talk to ghosts – a secret."

"I like that idea," Harper said. "Can we do that?" She turned to Jared, a hopeful expression on her face.

"Sure," Jared said. "If that will make you comfortable, I'm all for it. I'm also comfortable with you telling the truth, though. If you change your mind and want to come clean, I'll be right there with you."

"Thank you for that," Harper said. "Zander is right, though. I'm nervous. I don't remember the last time I was nervous, but I can't help myself. I'll be wearing weird clothes. This is our first trip together. I'm meeting an old friend of yours. It's ... daunting."

"I remember the last time you were nervous," Zander said. "It was when you two finally had your first date – which led to your first round of sex – and you both were messes. Who got you through that?"

"We did," Jared said.

"That's right, I did," Zander said, ignoring Jared. "You're going to be fine, Harp. I promise you that everything is going to work out. Jared has your back ... and if he doesn't, I'm only a phone call away."

Jared narrowed his eyes. "I think I can handle this," he said. "Besides, it's not all going to be strangers. The murder mystery is being held at the Stokes Hotel. It belongs to Josh's parents. They'll be there, too, along with a few other members of his family and maybe even some people we went to college with. She's going to be fine."

"Awesome," Zander said, grabbing three dresses from the pile and striding toward the closet. "Harp, I'm packing your dresses in Jared's garment bag to make things easier. Put all your naughty things in that small bag I got for you."

"Yes, sir," Harper grumbled, causing Jared to smirk. She moved to get up, but Jared stopped her with a hand on her hip. "What?"

"I promise you're going to have fun," Jared said. "Please don't be nervous. I know you can't help yourself, but … this is going to be great. It's our first official couple's trip. I know people and I'm a little nervous. I'm also really excited. I can't wait to introduce you to people."

"You have a wonderful way about you."

"Right back at you," Jared said, grabbing Harper's chin and planting a scorching kiss on her. "Now show me the naughty stuff before you put it in the bag. I want something good to dream about tonight."

"And that's my cue to leave," Zander said, moving toward the door. "Just for the record, I will be hopping into bed with the two of you tomorrow morning because it's my last Harper fix for a week. You can't stop me, so don't even try."

"Knock before you enter," Jared ordered.

"Cover your freaky nipples so I don't inadvertently stare," Zander shot back.

"I don't have freaky nipples!"

Harper raised her eyebrows as she got to her feet, chuckling as she watched Jared rub his chest. It appeared she wasn't the only insecure one.

JARED WOKE TO THE SOUND OF VOICES, INTERNALLY SIGHING when he realized Zander was not only in the room, but also on the opposite side of the bed. He pressed his eyes shut and pretended he was sleeping so he could listen for a few minutes.

"I think you're going to have a marvelous time," Zander said. "You'll be nervous for the first few minutes and then you'll relax and be the charmer we all know and love."

"No one has ever called me charming," Harper countered.

"I call you charming all of the time," Zander said. "Stop stressing yourself out. You're going to be a hit and Jared is going to be thrilled to show you off to his friends. You're very attractive. People will think he paid for the pleasure of your company you're so attractive."

"Are you insinuating I look like a hooker?"

Jared bit his lip to keep from laughing. There was something delightful about the way Harper and Zander interacted. As much as he wished he had her to himself more often, Jared would never try and get between Harper and Zander. They were magical in the way they loved one another.

"You don't look like a hooker," Zander replied. "I still maintain if you acted like a hooker in the bedroom Jared would like it, though."

"You're such a freak," Harper complained.

They were quiet for a few moments.

"You're going to be okay at work, right?" Harper asked. "You can handle Molly and Eric without too much difficulty, I'm sure. They've been fighting a lot lately, though."

"Yes, well, Molly is irritating and Eric has a bad attitude," Zander said, referring to GHI's other two employees. "They'll be fine. I'm actually looking forward to telling Eric you're spending the week with Jared at a sleazy hotel. He's trying to put his crush on you behind him and this will pretty much send him over the edge."

"It's not a sleazy hotel."

"It will be when I get done telling the story," Zander said. "Harp, I promise things are going to be fine. If we need you, we'll call you. You're only twenty minutes away."

"I know. It's just … I'm going to miss you. When was the last time we were apart this long?"

"I'll call you every day," Zander said. "In fact, since you're going to miss me so much, why don't we Skype in bed every morning? It will be fun. Just cover up Jared's nipples so they don't scare me."

Jared fought the urge to scowl.

"Okay," Harper said. "We'll Skype every morning."

"And if you have a fashion emergency, don't hesitate to call," Zander added. "I'll have my cell phone with me. I'll help you look like the princess you are."

"Thank you," Harper said, her voice low. "You're the best friend a girl could ever ask for."

"And I have beautiful nipples," Zander said. "Unlike your boyfriend who is eavesdropping while he's pretending to be asleep."

Jared forced out an exasperated sigh and rolled so he was facing Harper and Zander. They sat next to each other, their backs propped against the pillows, and studied him. "How did you know I wasn't sleeping?"

"You make little cooing noises when you're asleep," Zander answered. "It's very cute."

"I don't coo when I'm asleep." Jared glanced at Harper for help. "Tell him I don't coo."

"It's more of a whirring sound," Harper said. "It lulls me to sleep now. I love it."

"Well, I guess I can live with that," Jared muttered. "How much longer until we can hop in the shower and get moving?"

"Ten minutes."

"Fine," Jared said. "Wake me when you're done talking about my nipples."

FOUR

"This place is beautiful," Jared said a few hours later, slowing his truck so he could take in the breathtaking Stokes Hotel as he coasted onto the driveway. The grandiose estate was four stories high, square in design with gargoyles sitting at each corner, and highlighted by gray stones that allowed the building to cut an imposing figure against the Lake St. Clair backdrop. "I can't believe this place. I had no idea it would be like this."

"Haven't you ever been here before?" Harper asked, smiling as she watched Jared's reaction. He'd taken the entire trip in stride – including riding the ferry – but he couldn't mask his youthful exuberance. He really was excited. That made Harper happy and determined to make sure he had a good time.

"Josh told me about it when we were at college, but I guess I never understood what he was saying," Jared replied. "He said he grew up in a big house on an island. I was picturing a beach house for some reason. This place is a mansion. Heck, this place is four mansions."

"It's amazing," Harper agreed. "Zander and I used to come here from time to time when we were teenagers. He loved the art museum and I loved the water. We always used to stare at this place – it wasn't always a hotel like it is now – and dream about what it would be like to be rich enough to own a place this big.

"Zander's fantasy involved muscular pool boys and mine involved the world's biggest library," she continued. "We figured the house was big enough for us to live together and still get everything we both wanted."

"When did it become a hotel?" Jared asked, turning his attention back to the road so he didn't inadvertently career off the cobblestone driveway. "Josh didn't really talk about much of that."

"It was a big deal on the news a few years ago," Harper hedged. "I … well … the news reports said that the Stokes family was in financial trouble and the state was going to take the land so they had no choice but to turn it into a hotel.

"I guess they were hit hard by the economic downturn in the early part of the century and they lost a lot of the money they had put away and never fully recovered," she continued. "This is all gossip, mind you, but I believe there was also talk of the Stokes family losing more money in the bank collapse which came a few years after that."

"That's too bad," Jared said, pulling into the parking lot on the east side of the building. "I'll bet it was cool to live in a house that has forty bedrooms. That makes hide and seek fun."

"I think it sounds like overkill," Harper replied. "When Zander and I used to come out here we envisioned ourselves in stocking feet sliding across hardwood and marble floors and never running out of new places to investigate. We were kind of geeks."

"I think you guys are wonderful," Jared said, meaning every word. "Go on."

"Anyway, when we started really talking about it, though, the idea of a house this big seemed lonely," Harper said. "It's very ostentatious and gorgeous, but I think a home should feel cozy. You should feel comfortable in the space. How could you ever get comfortable in something this big?"

"That's a good point," Jared said. "What does your dream house look like?"

Harper shrugged. "I don't know. I like an older house that has electrical updates. I like the idea of being close to a river. I like the lake, don't get me wrong, but a river is more fun and gives you a more rural feeling. I want a big yard and garden. I just want something ... homey."

"I think that's a good dream," Jared said, killing the engine of his truck and reaching over to snag Harper's hand. "Are you ready for this?"

"I'll be fine," Harper said. "I'm sorry I was so nervous before. I feel a little silly about it now, but ... I don't want to embarrass you."

"Harper, you could never embarrass me," Jared said. "I like you just the way you are. That's why I couldn't stay away from you, if you remember correctly. People here are going to see exactly what I see: A beautiful woman they want to get close to. If someone tries to hit on you, though, I'm going to pop them. That includes Josh. They may want to get close to you, but I'm the only one allowed to get close to you."

Harper giggled. "Is Josh a ladies' man?"

"I think we all fancied ourselves ladies' men back in the day," Jared replied. "I'm not sure we realized how ridiculous we were, but he's a good guy. He'll hit on you to irritate me, however. Trust me. I wouldn't worry too much about it, though. It's all an act."

"Well, let's do this," Harper said, slapping her hands against her knees to motivate herself. "We're going to a murder mystery event and I have new clothes. This has disaster written all over it."

"You're so stinking cute," Jared said, cupping the back of Harper's head and pressing a soft kiss to her lips. "Stick with me," he whispered. "I'm going to give you the time of your life."

"JARED!"

Harper snapped her head to the top of the circular stairway and smiled when she saw the handsome man descending. His face was flushed with excitement as he approached Jared, and Harper took a step back to let the men greet each other on their own terms.

"I can't believe you're actually here," Josh said, giving Jared a one-armed man hug and grinning. "I never thought I would see the day. I missed you, man."

"I can't believe you live in this place," Jared said. "I thought you were exaggerating when you described it. Apparently not."

"I don't exaggerate," Josh said. "You're the one who exaggerates."

"That is such crap," Jared chuckled, smiling fondly at his friend. "I can't believe I'm saying this, but I missed you, too."

Josh Stokes was pretty much what Harper envisioned. He was tall like Jared, although his hair was blond instead of dark. He was well built and muscular, his jeans hugging his hips as he amiably chatted with his friend. Unlike the staff at the hotel, who were dressed in uniforms and stiff when greeting guests, Josh was friendly and welcoming. Harper instantly liked him.

"And who is this?" Josh asked, shifting his attention to Harper. "This can't be the girlfriend you were going on and on about over the phone, could it?"

"No," Jared deadpanned. "I picked her up on the street during the drive."

"Always the comedian," Josh said, shaking his head. "I'm Josh Stokes. You must be the famous Harper Harlow."

"I'm not sure I'm famous," Harper hedged, extending her hand in greeting. "The Harper Harlow part is correct, though."

"You are ... freaking hot," Josh said, grinning as he looked Harper up and down. "Jared always did like them beautiful."

"Um ... okay," Harper said, her cheeks burning.

"Leave her alone," Jared instructed, slipping his arm around Harper's waist. "She's mine. Keep your filthy hands to yourself."

"I can see why you're claiming her like a Neanderthal," Josh teased, beaming at Harper. "I can't believe you managed to get him to settle down. I thought for sure he would be a bachelor for life."

"I'm not sure he's settled down," Harper hedged.

"I am," Jared interjected. "I'm happily settled to boot. What about you? Do you have a lady love here this weekend?"

"I'm keeping my options open," Josh replied. "You know me. I can't settle down until I'm sure I've found the perfect woman. Since you've already locked the perfect woman up, I'll probably end up being a bachelor for life. It's a hard job, but somebody has to do it."

"Ha, ha," Jared intoned, rolling his eyes. "What are you doing these days?"

"Working for the family," Josh replied. "I do charity events and occasional business meetings. Most of the time I handle the hotel and put out employee fires and listen to complaining guests. It's all very boring.

"What about you, though?" he continued. "Is being a police detective everything you thought it would be? Whisper Cove can't be much of a hotbed of activity."

"You'd be surprised," Jared countered. "I've been in town two months and already solved two murders. I also met a certain blonde ... so I guess you could say life in Whisper Cove is better than I ever envisioned."

"Good for you," Josh said, slapping Jared's shoulder and laughing. "What about you, Harper? What do you do?"

"Oh, my life is pretty boring," Harper replied. "I basically run haunted tours with my best friend. We do those cemetery visits and stuff. It's not much, but it pays the bills."

Jared's eyes momentarily flashed and Harper felt a ball of guilt land in the pit of her stomach. It wasn't really a lie and yet it felt dishonest. She didn't know why she was being so evasive, but she couldn't help herself.

"That sounds fun," Josh said, his eyes lighting up. "You'll be great for the game."

"Yeah, about the game, I'm not sure we want to play," Jared said. "I'm a cop. That gives me an unfair advantage."

Josh derisively snorted. "I think you don't want to play because you don't want anyone else showing you up," he said. "The people coming this week take these murder mysteries very seriously. They have a club and they travel all over the U.S. attending these events. I'll bet they solve it before you even realize what's happening."

"I'll take that bet," Jared said, narrowing his eyes.

"I take it you guys are competitive," Harper said, smirking. "Does this mean I get to watch you thump your chests and secrete testosterone all week?"

"I'm not comfortable with that secreting testosterone thing," Jared answered. "I will be thumping my chest … but I'm waiting until we're alone in our room to do that."

Harper pressed her lips together and lowered her eyes, horrified by the mirthful expression on Josh's face. "Jared," she hissed, shifting uncomfortably.

"Oh, she's shy," Josh said, laughing. "I love her already. I'm going to steal her from you. I can't believe she's been so close and I didn't stumble across her first. I think it's a sign."

"It's definitely a sign," Jared said. "That sign reads 'closed.' She's mine. Don't go hitting on my girl. I'll have to beat you."

"Promises, promises," Josh said. "Well, come on. We'll get you two checked in and let you get settled. I have a surprise waiting for you upstairs that I think Harper is going to love."

"I CAN'T believe this," Harper said, exhaling heavily as she glanced around the humongous suite. "I … Jared, did you know they were going to give us one of the four corner rooms?"

Jared lifted his eyebrows and smirked as he watched Harper flit from one end of the suite to the other. She was enamored with the room and everything in it, including the antique furniture.

"I didn't know that corner rooms existed," Jared admitted. "I asked for a beautiful room because I wanted to impress you, but I was not expecting this. It's pretty nice, huh?"

"Nice?" Harper widened her eyes to almost comical proportions. "Nice? I feel like a princess."

"You're my princess," Jared said, snagging Harper around the waist and twirling her. He pressed her body against his and kissed her, loving the way she melted against him. When they finally separated, they were both out of breath. "Well, princess, what do you want to do first?" Jared had specific ideas, and he hoped Harper was up to the challenge.

"I want to check out the balcony."

Jared frowned. "I thought we would check out the bed first."

"Oh, we're going to do that," Harper said. "I want to check out the balcony first, though. Once we're in that bed, I know we're not coming up for hours."

"Okay," Jared conceded, linking his fingers with hers and letting her lead him to the ornate French doors on the far side of the room. "Let's check out the balcony."

Harper threw open the doors, her excitement contagious as she stepped through them. She gasped when the lake sprang into view and then sighed as she took in the rest of the surroundings. "Look at this."

Despite himself, Jared was impressed. "This is ... wow. I didn't know Michigan had views like this so far south."

"Can we hang out on the balcony after dark?" Harper asked, her eyes twinkling. "No one will be able to see us because we're isolated on the corner and ... well ... I've had specific fantasies about these balconies since I was old enough to have *those* kind of fantasies."

"Heart, you had me at fantasies," Jared teased, kissing the tip of her nose. "It's too bright to do that out here right now, though. I'm a cop. I would hate to have to arrest myself for lewd behavior."

"I know," Harper said.

"Does that mean we can check out the bed?" Jared was hopeful.

"That means we can check out that awesome claw foot tub that's big enough to swim in and take a bath," Harper countered. "Then we can check out the bed."

"Hey, there's nudity involved in both of those options," Jared said. "I'm up for whatever you want to do."

"Does that include bubbles?"

Jared grinned. "What's a bath without bubbles?"

"Boring," Harper said, shuffling excitedly toward the bathroom. "This is already the best vacation ever."

"It really is," Jared said, following her. "Let's take a bath. Bubble me up, baby."

FIVE

"I don't know if I should wear this."

Harper stood in front of the mirror and studied her black dress. It was a simple frock, boasting thin spaghetti straps, a modest neckline, and a skirt that ended three inches above her knees, but she still felt overdressed.

Jared shifted his tie knot into place as he looked her up and down. "You look amazing."

Harper lifted her blue eyes to Jared's and bit her lip. He'd never seen her unsure of herself in any situation. Her reticence now was cute. "I have an idea," Jared said, grabbing his cell phone off the table and punching in Zander's number.

Zander didn't bother with small talk. "Is she freaking out?"

Jared chuckled. "She looks like a dream and yet she doesn't think the dress looks good on her," he said. "I thought you could handle this situation."

"Absolutely," Zander said. "Put her on the phone."

Harper knit her eyebrows together and scowled as she took the phone from Jared. "He's exaggerating."

Jared smirked as he watched Harper talk to Zander, enjoying the way she fidgeted and twirled in front of the mirror. She had no idea how beautiful she looked, which was one of the things he liked best about her.

"I'm not being a pill, Zander," Harper snapped. "I just ... you know I have issues with dresses. Do you remember what happened at the senior dance when I wore that pink dress I found at the mall?"

Jared crossed his arms over his chest and patiently waited while Harper listened to whatever diatribe Zander launched into on the other end of the call.

"Oh, that's not true," Harper said. "That dress was beautiful. It wasn't doing me a favor when you stepped on it and it ripped resulting in no one seeing it. You're crazy."

After a few more minutes of sparring, Harper ended the call and handed Jared his phone.

"Better?" Jared asked.

"I guess," Harper hedged. "I'm not a big fan of you turning Zander into your ally and my enemy, though. He's my best friend."

"Which means you trust him to tell you the truth when you're still wondering if I'm schmoozing you to boost your ego," Jared said. "It's okay. That's how a relationship works. You look beautiful, though, and I don't want you thinking otherwise."

"And it's just dinner first, right?" Harper pressed. "We don't start the game right away, do we?"

"My understanding is that the game doesn't start right away," Jared replied. "That means you can enjoy your food – and get to know everyone – without your competitive side taking over."

"What is that supposed to mean?"

"You like to win," Jared said. "You can say whatever you want about playing the game because we're guests, but you want to win. I know you."

Harper frowned. "I hardly think ... ."

Jared held up his hand to cut her off. "I want to win, too," he said. "At first I thought the game was going to be a distraction that I didn't want when I could be holed up with you. Now I realize we can do both. With us working as a team, no one is going to be able to touch us."

Harper fought the urge to smile … and lost. "You know there aren't going to be any real ghosts here to help us win the game, right?"

Jared shrugged. "I know there's a really beautiful woman here to entertain me no matter what, so I think we're going to be okay."

"You're full of charm," Harper said, taking a step toward Jared so she could kiss his cheek. She wiped away her lipstick remains and smiled. "Thank you for being you."

"Oh, no," Jared countered. "Thank you for being you. Now, come on. I could use some appetizers. We worked up an appetite this afternoon."

"That was you," Harper said, laughing as Jared ushered her toward the door. "I've never seen anyone that excited to take a bath before."

"Just wait until it's time to take another one," Jared said. "I'm going to add more bubbles and see where the night takes us. I have a feeling it's going to be soapy Heaven."

"I can live with that."

"WOW," Harper said, exhaling heavily when she got a gander at the busy foyer. "Did you know they were going to invite so many people?"

Jared shrugged as he glanced around the room. "No, but it doesn't surprise me. They have forty rooms, right? This is supposed to be a charity event, so why not fill every room? Josh said that a lot of the people visiting go to murder mystery events all over the place. They treat it like a sport."

"I don't think murder mysteries are a sport," Harper said. "Of course, I don't think NASCAR is a sport either."

"Why not?" Jared asked. "I'm not a big NASCAR fan, but why don't you like it?"

"I don't care about it either way," Harper replied. "It's not a sport, though. It's a hobby. Basketball is a sport. Hockey and tennis are sports. NASCAR is driving. That's not a sport."

"I'll keep that in mind," Jared said, chuckling as he slipped his arm around Harper's waist. "Do you want something to drink?"

"Sure," Harper said. "I don't want to get drunk in case you try and take advantage of me, but a drink sounds nice."

"I don't need to get you drunk to take advantage of you," Jared scoffed. "I'm hot and manly. You want me to take advantage of you whether alcohol is involved or not."

"Now you sound like Zander," Harper said, smiling at the waiter as he stopped in front of the couple with a tray full of drink choices. "Um ... I just want a simple glass of wine. Is that what this is?"

The waiter nodded.

Harper took the drink while Jared opted for a whiskey sour. The couple made their way to the far side of the room so they could watch the crowd without feeling overwhelmed. They stood that way for almost ten minutes before Josh approached.

"You guys aren't fighting, are you?"

Jared was surprised. "Why would we be fighting?"

"I don't know," Josh said, his gaze bouncing between Harper and Jared. "I've been watching you. You haven't been talking and you've been paying attention to everyone else."

Jared chuckled. "That's strategy, man," he said. "We're trying to get a feeling for our opponents so we can win. Isn't first prize a weeklong stay in one of the corner suites? Harper loves the tub, by the way. You went above and beyond when giving us a room."

"I'm glad you like it," Josh said, breaking into a wide grin. "I wasn't sure if it would be your thing, but I wanted to give you a fair shot because most women love those rooms."

"It's beautiful," Harper said. "I used to come out here with my friend Zander when I was a teenager. We'd always stare at your house. It sounds weird to say now, but we absolutely loved it."

"Was Zander your boyfriend?" Josh asked.

"He's my best friend," Harper clarified. "We've never dated. We still live together, though."

Josh arched an eyebrow. "Your girlfriend lives with another man and you don't have a problem with it?"

"I don't have a problem with it," Jared said, knowing exactly what Josh was getting at. "He's gay, but that's beside the point. He and

Harper are ridiculously close. He's a fun guy – except when he's picking on my nipples."

Harper bit the inside of her cheek to keep from laughing.

"Your nipples?" Josh was puzzled. "Why does he care about your nipples?"

"You would have to meet him to understand," Jared explained. "Now that I know we're so close, hopefully we'll be able to meet up more often. I can come out here and you can come to Whisper Cove and meet Zander."

"Do all of the women in Whisper Cove look like Harper?" Josh looked hopeful.

"Oh, they broke the mold with her," Jared said, sympathetically patting Josh's shoulder. "You're fresh out."

"You are a cold man," Josh said, although his mischievous smile told Harper he was joking. "So, what are you guys doing over here? You know you can mingle with the other guests, right?"

"We're honestly happy watching everyone for right now," Jared replied. "You can learn a lot about a person from seeing how they interact when they think no one is looking."

"That's that cop thing you do," Josh said. "I've never liked it."

"I think it's cute," Harper said, slipping her arm around Jared's waist.

"She thinks it's cute," Jared said, beaming. "I'm going with her take on this, not your take."

"Whatever," Josh said, rolling his eyes. "Did you grow up in Whisper Cove, Harper?"

Harper nodded. "I was born there."

"Did you go to college?"

"I did," Harper confirmed, nodding. "Zander and I went to Central Michigan University together."

"So how did you end up back in Whisper Cove running ghost tours?"

"Oh, um ... ." Harper had no idea how to answer. She didn't want to admit her gift – even though she liked Josh – because it often made people uncomfortable. She also wasn't keen on lying. "It's one of those things that just happened."

Jared studied her for a moment, his face conflicted. "She's very good at what she does," he said finally. "She and Zander turn it into outright entertainment several times a week."

"So you work and live with Zander?" Josh asked. "That seems a bit … intense."

"You have no idea," Jared said. "They're extremely loud when they're around one another. I haven't seen them at work often, but I can imagine it gets … rowdy."

"I'll have you know that Zander and I are professionals," Harper said, making a face. "We don't get rowdy."

"Two nights ago you two came home covered in mud and arguing about nipples," Jared pointed out.

"Your nipples!" Harper's voice carried and a few people shifted their attention, causing Josh and Jared to snicker while Harper's cheeks turned crimson.

"Way to make a scene, Heart," Jared said, squeezing her hip. "If you were trying to go under the radar, I think you just lost your edge."

"Thanks to you," Harper muttered.

"Oh, my poor girl," Jared said, slinging an arm around her shoulders and kissing her forehead.

Josh watched, dumbfounded. "You really are off the market, aren't you?"

"I really am," Jared said, guileless. "That's what happens when you find a … magical … woman."

"Ugh. You've turned into a schmaltzy schmuck," Josh said, rolling his eyes. "I'm glad you're happy, but come on. What happened to the Jared I used to know? No offense, Harper, but Jared Monroe was quite the lothario back in the day."

"I'll bet," Harper said, smirking. "I could tell the minute I met him that he thought he was something special. He thought I should fall at his feet and worship."

"I didn't think that … and you kind of *did* do that all on your own," Jared said.

"Oh, whatever," Harper scoffed.

"Hey, I know what you were thinking the first time you saw me," Jared said. "It was written all over your face."

"I thought you were kind of full of yourself," Harper said.

"I know," Jared said. "It was written all over your face. I still managed to win you over."

"After arresting me."

Josh stilled, surprised. "You arrested her?"

Harper realized her mistake too late. "Oh, um ... ."

"My very first case in Whisper Cove was a murder," Jared explained. "A girl's body washed up on the beach. Harper and Zander decided to help with the investigation because their assistant Molly was a student at St. Clair Community College and they were worried about her. I caught Harper trespassing at the victim's house when she was investigating."

As far as lies go, it was a good one. It wasn't completely isolated from the truth, and it didn't leave Harper looking like a crazy person.

"Oh, so you're a busybody," Josh said, laughing. "I like that. Did he really arrest you?"

"Yes."

"I didn't arrest you," Jared clarified, smiling at the memory. "I took you into custody and immediately released you when your mother and Zander showed up screaming for an end to your inhumane incarceration."

"Oh, that's so cute," Josh said. "When you guys have kids you'll be able to tell that story to them and it will be one of those family tales that lives on forever."

Harper and Jared both shifted, talk of kids making them uncomfortable.

"Oh, sorry," Josh said, realizing what he'd said. "It's too soon for that."

"Way too soon," Jared said, although he risked a glance at Harper to see what she was thinking. Her face was unreadable. "We already have a child as it is. His name is Zander and he even climbs into bed with us to tell us about his day."

Josh snorted. "Please tell me you have a photo of that."

"Thankfully, no," Jared said.

"Zander takes selfies while you're still sleeping all of the time,"

Harper countered. "I don't let him put them on Facebook because of my bedhead, though."

"I think your bedhead is cute," Jared said. "I'm going to break Zander's phone when I see him next."

"He backs up the photos in an online cloud," Harper said. "We're stuck with them."

"Well, that's great," Jared said, rolling his neck until it cracked. "So tell us about the game. How does it work?"

"It's pretty simple really," Josh said. "After dinner everyone will go into the library for a small speech by my father – he really gets off on being the center of attention – and then a body will just happen to be discovered tomorrow morning."

"Oh, I thought the game started tonight," Jared said, mildly disappointed.

"No, my father wants to lull people into a false sense of security before dropping a body," Josh answered. "He loves the drama involved with this whole thing. I can't explain it.

"Most of the workers here are straight workers, but we've intermixed actors in, too," he continued. "Some of the staff wanted to act and some didn't, so we left it up to them. Most of them are playing and they're excited."

"So are the guests suspects?" Harper asked.

"The guests are suspects in the fact that a handful of them aren't really guests," Josh replied. "They're paid actors and part of a traveling mystery group. You're not supposed to be able to tell who is an actor and who is a guest. If you figure it out, though, tell me. I'm curious if they can fool a real cop."

"That almost sounds more fun than the murder mystery," Jared said, tightening his arm around Harper's waist. "How soon until dinner?"

"Any second now," Josh said. "They'll make an announcement. You should be happy. It's prime rib and all the fixings."

"You had me at prime rib," Jared said. "I … ." He broke off when a stately man moved to the head of the foyer and cleared his throat. "Oh, I think it's starting."

"Dinner is served," the man said.

"That's Trask Daniels," Josh said, wrinkling his nose. "He's been a butler for us since before we turned the house into a hotel. He has absolutely no sense of humor, so if you want to mess with him, I encourage you to do so."

Jared grinned. "Let the games begin."

SIX

"That was the best meal I've had in I don't know how long," Jared said, his fingers linked with Harper's as they walked around the Stokes Hotel property after dinner. "I'm not joking. I think I ate an entire cow."

Harper giggled as she glanced at the night sky, tilting her head back and groaning when her own stomach lurched. "It's a good thing I didn't wear pants," she said. "If I did, they would be unbuttoned right now."

"Very cute," Jared said, spinning Harper so he could plant a kiss on her lips. "Not that I'm complaining about spending time with you, but we could be up in our room right now letting dinner digest instead of walking around. Upstairs we could be naked, too, so I think it has the edge."

Harper rolled her eyes. "I need to walk a little bit after that dinner we ate," she explained. "If we go upstairs now, I don't care what you say, we're going to pass out instead of doing anything fun. This way we'll get a second wind."

"I like the way your mind works," Jared said, giving her another kiss before releasing her and bending over. "I seriously ate too much. I haven't been this stuffed since Thanksgiving – and then we dealt with it by planting ourselves on the couch and watching football."

"You don't have to stay with me," Harper offered. "I'll probably only be twenty minutes if you want to go back up to the room and rest."

"I'm not leaving you alone with a murderer on the loose," Jared said, wrinkling his nose. "Get real."

"It's a fake murderer."

"And you're my real girlfriend who I don't want to be separated from," Jared shot back. "I'm not leaving you."

Harper pushed out a dramatic sigh. "Fine. We can go back to the room. Don't come crying to me when we fall asleep before playing games on the balcony, though."

"We don't have to go inside," Jared said. "I was just complaining because ... well ... I thought you liked it given your relationship with Zander."

"Ha, ha," Harper intoned. "I'm telling him you said that."

"Make sure you also tell him my nipples are better than his nipples."

"I'll get right on that," Harper said, turning her attention to the expansive lawn. The sun was long gone, but the heat of the day remained. Summer was officially here, and Harper was glad to shake off the doldrums of winter – and a shaky spring – to embrace the warmth. After autumn, summer was her favorite season. "It's beautiful out here. Whisper Cove is pretty at night, too, but seeing the stars against the water like this is magical."

"You're magical," Jared said, wrapping his arm around her waist from behind and rubbing his nose against her neck. "Did you have a good time tonight?"

"It was nice," Harper said. "I didn't really understand what some of the people were saying, but ... they seemed mostly normal."

Jared chuckled, his mind wandering back to the odd dinner conversation. "Those mystery people definitely have some quirks," he said. "I like the guy who carries his own whiskey in a flask because he's convinced someone is going to try and poison him because he's so good at solving these mystery events."

"He says he's won seven of them," Harper said. "Of course, Tara and Tim Lockhart, who happened to be sitting next to me, say he cheated. They also think he's a pompous blowhard."

Jared smirked. "He had that air about him, didn't he?"

"I think they're fine," Harper said. "Everyone has different interests. While I think a murder mystery game sounds fun for a change of pace, I can't see myself wanting to do it all of the time. We've had enough murders recently."

"We definitely have," Jared agreed, studying her profile. They hadn't talked much about her ordeal at the hands of a former classmate several weeks before. He decided to let her open up about it at her own pace and not press her until she was ready. She'd barely mentioned it, though. "I heard an update about Jim, if you're interested, that is."

Harper shifted and for a moment Jared thought he saw worry flitting across her features. It was gone before he could be sure. "Please tell me he's not going to get off on a technicality or something."

"He's definitely not going to get off on a technicality," Jared replied. "He's locked up in the county jail until trial and then he's going to move to a prison facility. There's no way he can get off."

Jim Stone was Harper's former schoolmate and nemesis. After a local teenager showed up dead in Whisper Cove's park, Jared and Harper investigated and found that Jim was using impressionable teens to move drugs and he wasn't above murder to keep his secret. Stone kidnapped Harper with the intent to force her into submission at an isolated location, but she managed to escape and subdue him. She was still kind of shaky after a frightening run through the woods with a killer on her tail.

"What's the update?"

"He's trying to offer testimony against the teenagers for a lighter sentence, but the prosecutor shot him down," Jared answered. "He's not happy."

"Good. I hope he's miserable," Harper muttered.

"I'm sure he is," Jared said. "You're not miserable because of him, are you?"

Harper was surprised by the question. "Why would you ask that?"

"That's not an answer," Jared prodded. "You never talk about it. It's okay to be upset ... worried even. I'm here if you need me."

"Thank you for the offer, but I'm really fine."

Jared cocked a dubious eyebrow.

"I'm mostly fine," Harper conceded. "In case you've forgotten, I knew Jim was evil long before he kidnapped me."

"I haven't forgotten," Jared said, smiling despite himself. "I've learned to trust your instincts. You were definitely right about Stone. You had a nightmare a few nights ago, though. Was that about him?"

"That was about a ghost sneaking into Zander's room and putting him in mismatched socks while he slept."

"Harper ... ."

"I'm not joking," Harper said. "Zander was very upset in the dream ... and that's why he didn't notice when Jim kidnapped me. It was a dream, though, Jared. It wasn't real life. I survived. We're together. Everything is okay."

"I don't want to force you to talk if you don't want to do it," Jared said. "I also don't want you sweeping all of this under the rug because you think you're being a burden ... or somehow silly. You're very strong, but it's okay to let me take care of you if you're upset."

"Is that part of those relationship rules you're always spouting?"

"It is," Jared confirmed.

"I'm honestly fine," Harper said. "If I need you, I know where to find you."

"Right by your side."

"Right by my side," Harper said, tilting her chin up so she could kiss the corner of Jared's mouth. "Do you mind if we take a ten-minute walk before going back to our room? I'd like this dinner to settle before we shake it up again."

"I think that's a great idea," Jared said, tweaking Harper's nose. "Do you want to walk down to the lake?"

"Actually ... ." Harper broke off and swiveled her head, racking her brain for a memory location before pointing toward a spot over Jared's shoulder. "Let's walk that way."

"You want to walk to the woods?" Jared wasn't thrilled with the suggestion. "Why do you want to go to the woods?"

"I don't want to go to the woods," Harper replied. "They have a family cemetery over there and I want to look at it."

"A cemetery is worse than the woods, Heart," Jared complained.

"Not this one," Harper argued. "Zander and I saw it when we were younger and it's only a few graves. It's closed in by a fence with an iron gate, but it's made up of tiny mausoleums and it has beautiful stained glass windows – at least it did ten years ago."

"Okay," Jared said, giving in and taking her hand. "Let's check out the cemetery. You know you're going to have to give me something really special in return for hanging out with you in a cemetery, right?"

Harper snorted. "What did you have in mind?"

"I was hoping for another bath."

"Blech. I don't want to see your nipples again. They'll give me nightmares."

"I'm going to kill Zander," Jared muttered.

"WELL, IT'S DEFINITELY A CEMETERY," JARED SAID TEN MINUTES later, his gaze bouncing around the neatly kept parcel of land. "I don't understand what the deal is with these tiny buildings."

"It's because of the lake," Harper explained, her fingertips tracing the pattern on one of the ornate windows. "If there should ever be a flood or catastrophic weather event, the bodies would risk being washed away if they were planted beneath the ground. That's why they have all of these mausoleums instead. The bodies are entombed above ground."

"That is ... still weird," Jared said, although he was less creeped out than a few minutes before. "I thought maybe they had the buildings so people could hang out in them."

"Like clubhouses?"

"You're not very cute right now, just for the record," Jared said. "I've never seen anyone have an actual cemetery on their property."

"Harsens Island isn't very big," Harper pointed out. "They have a community cemetery on the other side of the island, but since the Stokes family was the richest one here, it probably made sense to have their own so they didn't have to mingle with the little people."

"How?"

Harper shrugged. "When people have money they like to spend it on weird things," she replied. "I think cemeteries are beautiful – and I'm not just saying that because I spend so much time in them – but I wouldn't want one on my property. I've seen *Poltergeist,* and that way leads to spooky clown dolls and trees that eat people."

"And you're back to being cute," Jared said, tickled by her take on life. "I've been considering asking Josh about his family's money problems, but that somehow feels invasive. On the flip side, it kind of feels callous to ignore the situation. What do you think?"

"I would let him bring it up to you if he wants to talk about it," Harper answered. "If you ask him he might think you're prying. You guys haven't been in regular touch so I think it would be out of place if you mentioned it out of the blue."

"That's probably true," Jared. "You're wise and adorable."

"I know," Harper said, shooting him a flirtatious wink.

"By the way, if you want to tell Josh what you really do for a living, I think he would not only understand but enjoy talking about it," Jared said. "I saw how uncomfortable you were when he asked you how you ended up back in Whisper Cove after college. You're a terrible liar – which is a good thing – but I honestly think you're overreaching on this one. Josh would be fine with it."

"I know," Harper said. "It's just … people always look at me differently when they find out what I can do."

"I don't."

"But you did," Harper said.

"When?"

"When we first met I could tell you thought I was attractive," Harper said, choosing her words carefully. "That didn't last long once Mel told you I thought I could see ghosts. You thought I was certifiable after that and wanted as much distance between us as possible."

Jared opened his mouth to argue and then snapped it shut. She wasn't wrong. "Okay," he conceded. "I questioned your sanity a little bit after Mel told me what you could do. It didn't take long for me to realize you were telling the truth, though.

"And, if we're being honest, part of me wanted to believe you from the start," he continued. "I'm a practical guy, though. I didn't believe in ghosts and the supernatural so I had a hard time wrapping my head around it. In the grand scheme of things, I came around really quickly."

"You did, and I'm thankful for that," Harper acknowledged. "I would just prefer a week where I don't have to explain that I see and talk to ghosts. I want to be normal this week. Are you okay with that?"

"I'm okay with anything you do," Jared said, extending his hand. "Now I want to be okay with what you do in that big bathtub."

Harper took his hand and smiled. "I have a feeling you're going to cover me with bubbles and then use me as a waterslide."

Jared barked out a laugh. "I love the way your mind works."

HARPER WAS BEING CHASED. SHE WAS LOST IN A DREAM – AND on some level she realized that – but that didn't stop her heart from hammering as the shadowy figure behind her closed in.

She scampered toward the stairs, realizing they were the ones that led to the main foyer of the Stokes Hotel, and glanced over her shoulder when she was convinced better lighting would reveal her stalker. It didn't. He was still nothing but a black mass and angry words. Harper didn't recognize the voice as he screamed about making her his personal property, and she was so fixated on trying to make out facial features she missed the top step and tumbled down the winding staircase, landing on the marble floors below with a sickening thud.

Harper turned swiftly – imagined dream pain minimal compared to the real thing she'd experienced when she jumped out of a moving vehicle weeks before – and found a black hand reaching out for her.

She opened her mouth to scream and instead bolted upright to a sitting position in her hotel room. It was dark, dawn still hours away, and her heart raced as she tried to understand the dream.

"What's wrong?" Jared murmured, shifting in the bed next to her. "Did you have a bad dream?"

"It's okay," Harper said, shaking her head. "I ... fell down the stairs in my dream and woke myself up when I tried to catch myself."

"I'll catch you," Jared said, slipping his arm around her waist and tugging her head to his bare chest. "Go back to sleep, Heart. We have a big day ahead of us."

"Uh-huh."

"It's okay," Jared whispered, stroking the back of her head. "I'm right here."

Despite his statement, Harper was convinced she would have trouble drifting off again. She was wrong.

SEVEN

J ared woke early the next morning, taking a moment to bask in Harper's warmth as she slumbered with her head on his shoulder and then glanced down at her quiet form. He usually didn't get a chance to enjoy mornings with her because Zander was already in bed with them when he woke up. As annoying as he found the situation, he was surprised to realize he almost missed the sound of their low murmurs and whispers as they tried not to wake him.

Jared traced lazy circles across the back of Harper's neck, studying her blond highlights and listening to her soft sighs as she slept. He could spend the entire day exactly like this and be happy.

As if on cue his stomach growled, causing Harper to shift.

"So much for the perfect morning," Jared muttered, forcing a smile when Harper tipped her chin in his direction. "Good morning."

"Morning," Harper murmured, struggling to get her bearings. "What time is it?"

"It's still early," Jared said. "We have two hours until we have to be downstairs for breakfast and the first murder."

"Is there going to be more than one murder?" Harper asked, making a comical face as she yawned. "I guess I'm not up on the rules of this thing."

"I'm sure we'll figure it out as we go along," Jared said. "In fact, if you wanted to go downstairs for breakfast and then turn around and come back for a nap and skip the murder mystery, I would be fine with that."

"We have to play," Harper said. "That's why we're here. It's not fair to Josh to skip out on the game."

"I thought we were here to spend time alone and cuddle," Jared said, tickling her bare ribs and drawing her close so they could snuggle. "I love how warm you are. I love how soft these sheets are. I … really am hungry."

Harper giggled. "I guess we should get up and start getting ready." She said the words but didn't make a move to leave her toasty spot.

Jared brushed her hair away from her face and met her blue eyes with a concerned look. "You had a nightmare last night. I just remembered."

"It was fine," Harper said, rolling her eyes. "There's no reason to get up in arms about it. It was just a dream. It wasn't even Jim this time."

"What was it?"

"It was a dream, Jared," Harper chided. "It was nothing."

"Then tell me about it," Jared pressed. "If it's nothing, you shouldn't have a problem sharing it with the group."

"Fine," Harper said, her eyes flashing as she tried to put a little distance between them. Jared kept her snugly against his chest and patiently waited for her dream retelling. "It's really nothing," she said, giving up and collapsing back against him. "I was running down a long hallway and I kept looking over my shoulder. I got to a set of stairs and realized I was here … I mean, in my dream, I was in the Stokes Hotel.

"Anyway, I was so busy looking behind me because I wanted to see who was chasing me I tripped and fell down the stairs," she continued. "When I turned there was a hand coming toward me and that's when I woke up."

Jared kept one arm around Harper's waist as he rubbed his thumb against her cheek. "Do you know who was chasing you?"

"I think it was you," Harper said. "You wanted another bath."

Jared cracked a smile even though he wasn't sure he wanted to let her off the hook. "That shows what you know," he said. "We're getting clean in that huge shower this morning."

"Oh, good. I love variety."

"Who was chasing you in the dream?" Jared asked, refusing to let Harper brush away his worry. "Was it Jim? You said it wasn't, but if it wasn't him, who was it?"

"I couldn't see his face," Harper replied, her expression earnest. "I am honestly perfectly fine."

"I know you are," Jared said, pressing his lips to her forehead. "It's okay to be rattled, though. It doesn't mean you're not the strongest woman in the world. It means you had something bad happen to you and you're still grappling with it."

"I'm fine."

"You're going to be better than fine," Jared said, giving in and embracing the fun of their morning. "You're going to be throwing a party in my honor in exactly five minutes." He offered her a long and sultry kiss. "You'll definitely be able to remember my face when I'm done with you."

"Less talking and more doing," Harper prodded.

"Seriously, I love the way you think."

"I THINK we're late," Harper said, frowning when she saw the empty foyer from the top of the stairs. "I don't think people are going to like it if we're late." She scurried down the stairs and hurried in the direction of the dining room. "I blame you."

Jared's grin was lazy as he followed her. The only reason he bothered to keep up was because she refused to let go of his hand. "Harper, I'm sure they're going to have enough food for us to eat when we get there. There's no reason to freak out."

"I'm not freaking out."

"You're close."

"I am not."

"You are so."

"Are you two always like this when you're late for breakfast?" Josh asked, stepping into the spot in front of the dining room doorway and fixing Harper and Jared with an amused look. "You sound like a squabbling brother and sister. That might bode well for me since I want to steal you away from Jared, Harper."

Jared narrowed his eyes and scowled. "If we were brother and sister we would be arrested for what we just did in the shower. That's why we're late."

"Jared!" Harper was horrified, and when Jared shifted his challenging eyes from Josh to Harper he realized the ramifications of what he'd said "I'm so sorry."

"It's my fault," Josh said smoothly, stepping in to protect his friend. "We were always very competitive and things often got out of hand. I pushed him on purpose because I thought it would be funny. I think both of us forgot someone else was involved in this equation."

"I'm really sorry," Jared said. "You live with Zander, though, and he once told you he waited until he was completely naked to dump a guy because his ... you know ... curved to the right and he had a Charley horse and couldn't possibly curve to the left to compensate."

"That was a great story," Josh said. "I really need to meet this Zander guy."

"What does that have to do with anything?" Harper asked, incredulous.

"I'm just saying you should be used to men saying absolutely asinine things about sex," Jared said.

"The difference is that Zander isn't telling sex stories about me," Harper pointed out. "As far as he's concerned, I don't have lady parts. I'm like a Barbie doll."

"You do have a few things in common with a Barbie doll," Jared said, his mind wandering. "Of course, you're anatomically correct, so that's a big bonus."

"You're going to have something in common with a Ken doll if you're not careful," Harper warned, wagging a finger for emphasis.

Jared caught the finger and pressed it to his lips. "I am truly sorry. I won't let it happen again. It was rude and disrespectful."

"It was funny, though," Josh said. "Of course, I could just think it's funny because you're in trouble and now I have a shot with your girl."

"Don't make me beat you," Jared warned.

"Wow," Harper intoned, wriggling her eyebrows. "This must be what it's like to have brothers."

Jared hung his head, sheepish. "I really am sorry."

"You're going to owe me," Harper said. "Apparently I owe my mother a thank you for letting me be an only child."

"I'll thank her for that, too," Jared said, slinging an arm over Harper's shoulders. "This way Josh can't get anyone even remotely close to you and I win."

"Yes, that's exactly what I was thinking," Harper said dryly.

"Come on," Josh said. "Breakfast is ready and then the game is set to begin. My father is in his element."

"Is this the first time you've done something like this?" Harper asked, following Josh into the ornate dining room. Since there were so many people the tables remained separated and the trio settled at an empty one so they could continue their discussion without interruption.

"It is," Josh confirmed. "My dad was against it when I suggested it, but we need ways to beef up business. I'm sure you heard about some of our ... troubles."

Jared and Harper exchanged a look.

"Harper knew a little bit about it because she's local, but I wasn't aware that anything had changed until we came up here," Jared said. "I'm sorry things aren't going well."

"When it first happened, it was a real blow," Josh said. "I didn't realize how bad things were. All my father said was that they lost money in investments. I thought we were more diversified than we were. This place is expensive to keep in operation and the upkeep is ... big."

"Is that why you moved home?"

"That's one of the reasons," Josh confirmed. "I've always loved this place. I like living on an island, and with this one you're really not very far away from civilization. I can take a boat and hit the mainland in twenty minutes if I feel like it.

"I had a choice to make and it wasn't easy," he continued. "My father was at his wit's end and had no idea what to do. He's never had to do anything but sit back and collect on the investments. I had a business degree and an idea. He wasn't happy, but he literally didn't have another choice."

"Are you considering hosting regular murder mystery weekends?" Harper asked.

"This is a test run," Josh confirmed. "In fact ... um ... I was hoping you guys would spend more time watching the guests to see if they're having a good time than actually participating in the murder mystery. I'd also like to know how the staff is handling things. Some of them have been reticent regarding the changes. I know it's a lot to ask …"

"Don't worry about it," Jared said, waving off Josh's concerns. "Harper is a little competitive, but I'm sure she'll be happy watching everyone else play."

"*I'm* a little competitive?" Harper challenged.

"Fine. I'm competitive, too," Jared said. "Still, we'll have a good time just hanging out and watching. Is there anything else you want us to do?"

"I don't know," Josh replied, rubbing the back of his neck. "Can you think of other events that would help put this place on the map?"

"I don't know anything about running a hotel, man," Jared said. "I'm sorry."

Harper's hand shot up and Josh and Jared chuckled as they locked eyes.

"I think Harper has an idea," Josh said.

"She's the top student in my class," Jared said. "Harper, what is your idea?"

"You can run haunted events," Harper offered, squirming in her seat. "You have a cemetery on the property and you're close to the woods. The house is isolated and you can do creepy murders in the fall when people are taking color tours.

"There's not a lot you can do in the winter because of the weather and how hard it is to get to the island, but I bet you could try booking the hotel out for entire weekends for one event," she continued. "You could do Viking themed dinners, or hunting is big in this area so you could do those strange meat dinners I've read about."

"How do you know about all of this?" Jared asked, surprised and impressed.

"And how did you just whip it out like that?" Josh asked. "Seriously, those are great ideas. What else have you got?"

"Well, I don't know about your father's political leanings, but Zander always complains that there aren't enough gay-centric events in this area," Harper said. "What about a special weekend with spa people? Zander absolutely loves a good massage, steam, and facial."

Jared snorted. "That's also a great idea. I'm not sure Mr. Stokes would appreciate forty Zanders running around, though."

"I'm in charge," Josh said. "I agree with Jared. That's another fabulous idea."

"You could also do beach party themes ... ooh, you could do a *Jaws* theme in the summer because you're on the water," Harper said, enjoying herself immensely.

"I think you've created a monster," Jared said, leaning back in his chair. "I think you missed your calling, Heart. You should've been a party planner."

"You definitely picked a good one," Josh said. "If I wasn't jealous before I would be now."

"I picked the best one," Jared said, smiling fondly at Harper. "She's mine, though. You missed out and now you have to live with it."

"I hear you have weird nipples," Josh said. "Maybe if I show her mine she'll trade up."

Jared's smile tipped upside down. "I'm seriously going to kill Zander."

EIGHT

"We're never going to want to leave this place," Harper said an hour later, pushing her clean plate away and leaning back in her chair. "I cannot remember the last time I ate this well two meals in a row."

"I cooked dinner and breakfast for you this week," Jared pointed out.

"And they were lovely," Harper said. "You didn't cook prime rib and homemade omelets, though. I even got to pick out as many things as I wanted for the omelet. I think this place might be Heaven."

Jared chuckled as he wiped the corners of his mouth and shifted his attention to Josh. "I can't believe you're not fat with all this food available at every meal."

"It gets old after a while," Josh said. "Believe it or not, there are days when I'm perfectly happy with my bowl of cereal. Of course, I've upgraded from Fruity Pebbles to Raisin Bran because I'm a grownup, but some habits die hard."

"I guess so," Jared said. "How long do we have until the body drops?"

"Why? Are you trying to decide if you have enough time to sneak upstairs for another shower?" Josh teased.

"Oh, man." Harper covered her eyes with her hand. "I'm never going to live this down."

"You had to embarrass me, didn't you?" Jared asked, making a face. "My girl gave you thirty ideas for theme weekends and you paid her back with snark. It's pitiful."

"I'm sorry," Josh said, holding his hands up in a placating manner. "That was uncalled for. I can't seem to help myself."

"Try," Jared said. "Harper, stop hiding your face. No one knows but the three of us and Josh is going to stop bringing it up, aren't you?"

"Of course," Josh said, although his eyes were mischievous. "I would never want to embarrass Jared."

"You're embarrassing me," Harper pointed out. "Jared wants to thump his chest and crow, but he's holding back because he doesn't want to upset me. I'm not an idiot."

"You're definitely not an idiot," Josh said, amused despite Harper's tone. "I want one of you. I really do. You're so ... cute." He reached out to pinch Harper's cheek, but Jared slapped his hand away.

"Don't even think about it," Jared chided. "She's mine. She's going to stay mine. She would never fall for the likes of you."

"Yes, but I own the house with the tub and shower she likes so much," Josh reminded Jared.

"Harper can't be bought," Jared said. "Right, Heart?"

"I don't know," Harper said primly. "If he has a box of those chocolates they left on our pillows last night, I might be able to be bought. I know I can buy Zander for a month straight if I take some of those home."

"Consider it done," Josh said, smirking at Jared's hangdog expression. "After all the ideas you've given me today, I think a box of chocolates is the least I can do."

"I'll still beat you if you don't stop hitting on her," Jared threatened.

"Sometimes you just have to put up with a beating if something is worth the pain," Josh teased, pushing himself up from his chair. "You guys have time for another mug of coffee ... or more food if you haven't had enough. The murder mystery will start in about forty minutes, and I have to check on a few things beforehand."

"We'll see you later," Jared said. "Good luck."

"Thanks," Josh replied. "I think I'm going to need it."

"LOOK AT THIS," HARPER SAID, HER VOICE BARELY A WHISPER as she walked into the Stokes Hotel library twenty minutes later. The body was supposed to be discovered in the distinguished room relatively soon and Harper wanted to see it before everyone descended and ruined the ambiance. "I've never seen this many books in my life."

"I think this must be what the inside of your head looks like," Jared said, his eyes wide as he took in the two-story room. Every wall was covered with bookshelves and every shelf was packed to the brim with antique books. The shelves had wrought iron ladders attached and they slid the length of the shelves. "This really is beautiful."

"Now this is a room I would like," Harper said, giggling when her voice echoed. "Of course, you could fit our entire house in this place and still have room for Zander's ego."

"What do you think all of these books are?" Jared asked, pulling a leather tome from the shelf and glancing inside. "I think this is Latin."

Harper glanced over his shoulder and nodded. "I think it's a Latin textbook. I can't be sure, though. The only Latin book I ever saw was in a poetry class I took in college."

"I can't picture you in a poetry class," Jared said, slapping the book shut and returning it to the shelf. "You seem like more of a horror girl, if you ask me. King ... Koontz ... those types of things."

"I do love a scary novel," Harper admitted. "I took poetry because Zander was insistent that he was going to learn how to write it to attract men. We read and wrote it for the class, and I barely passed."

Jared snickered. "Please tell me you have these poems hidden away at your house somewhere."

Harper averted her eyes. "Nope. I lost them years ago."

Jared didn't believe that for a second. "Zander will find them for me," he said. "I'll just bet he will do a dramatic reading for me, too."

"Ugh. Don't you dare," Harper said. "My poetry was terrible."

"How was Zander's?"

"He got stuck on the 'roses are red, violets are blue, look in my pants and you'll find something to surprise you' vein of poetry," Harper answered.

Jared's laugh was loud enough to fill the entire room just when the butler Trask entered.

"Do you need something?" Trask asked, his gaze busy as he looked Harper and Jared up and down. Apparently he wasn't impressed. "The mystery won't start for fifteen minutes."

"We're here for the ambiance," Harper replied, wrinkling her nose. "It's delightful."

"I see," Trask said. "I believe you're Josh's friend from college, right? Mr. Monroe?"

"I am," Jared confirmed, narrowing his eyes as he tried to get a handle on Trask's attitude. "I understand you've been working for the Stokes family for quite some time."

"Since Josh was five," Trask answered. "This house has been my home for the better part of my life."

"It's a hotel now," Harper pointed out. "Do you still live here?"

"I do," Trask said, walking to the bookshelf and pushing in the book Jared handled so it lined up with the other items on the shelf. "Hopefully this hotel thing will be a temporary measure."

"Don't you like the house being turned into a hotel?" Jared asked.

"Of course not," Trask sniffed. "It's undignified. This is a grand home. It's a showplace. It is not a spot for wayward travelers and … derelicts … to hang their hats for a night. The house was meant to house the finest family in the area. It certainly wasn't meant to be a place where people pretend to murder others for sport."

Harper pursed her lips to keep from laughing, Trask's outrage amusing her. Jared was merely puzzled.

"If you hate it so much, why not find another job?" Jared asked. "I have a feeling the hotel is going to be sticking around for some time. Josh made it sound as if this is going to be a permanent business."

"Nothing is permanent, Mr. Monroe," Trask said. "This sad chapter in a great house's history will not last. You can be sure of that."

"You're a real charmer, aren't you?" Jared wasn't amused in the least with Trask's attitude.

"I am a professional," Trask said. "I'm sure you don't understand what that means."

"You'd be surprised what I understand," Jared said. "What you should understand is that Josh is doing the best that he can to save this place. It's not some personal slap at you. It's business, and I think Josh can turn this place into a real moneymaker if he's given the tools to do it."

"Of course *you* would think that," Trask said. "You're a police officer, correct?"

"Yeah. So?"

"While I believe you have an important job to do, you cannot possibly understand the history of this house," Trask said. "It's out of your area of expertise. You should excel at the mystery game, though. I would think you'd have a leg up."

"Wow," Jared muttered, turning his attention to Harper. "Do you want to hang out with Mr. Friendly or go somewhere else until the fun begins?"

"I'm actually curious why you would go around telling people all of this when you're supposed to be working for the Stokes family," Harper said, her eyes dark as they fixed on Trask. "They're trying to build this into a business and they need strong word of mouth to do that. It seems to me that you're working against Josh's efforts. Why would he keep you here if that's the case?"

"Josh was always a good boy and he's turned into a charming man," Trask replied. "That doesn't mean he's lord of the manor."

"I think he *is* lord of the manor," Harper countered, crossing her arms over her chest. She clearly didn't like Trask any more than Jared did. "My understanding is that he's in charge of all of this. Doesn't that make him your boss?"

"You run haunted cemetery tours, right?" Trask asked, his tone derisive. "Do you really think you have the knowledge base to be involved in this conversation?"

"Hey!" Jared barked, taking a step forward. "What's your problem?"

"I'm sure I don't have a problem," Trask replied, flicking a piece of imaginary lint from his shoulder. "I think you must be confused."

"Is something going on here?"

Jared turned his attention to the doorway where Linden Stokes, Josh's father, hovered. "Nothing is going on," Jared said. "How are you, Mr. Stokes? I didn't really get a chance to talk to you last night. Thank you so much for inviting us."

"I was happy to see you, too," Linden said, his smile welcoming as his eyes darted worriedly in Trask's direction. "It's been a long time. You're certainly not the rabble rouser you were back then."

"I hope not," Jared said, smirking. "Josh isn't either."

"No, he's grown into a fine man," Linden said. "I understand you have, too. You work at the Whisper Cove Police Department, right?"

Jared nodded.

"How did you end up there?"

"I really wanted to work for a bigger department but there weren't a lot of openings," Jared explained. "I thought I could start at Whisper Cove and work my way to another department in a few years."

"That sounds smart," Linden said. "Whisper Cove is a beautiful area."

"It is," Jared agreed. "Now that I'm there and I've seen all that the town has to offer, I'm not sure I want to move on to a bigger job. I haven't made any decisions yet, but I think the smaller job might be the perfect job now that I'm in it."

"I think your decision hinges on Ms. Harlow more than the job," Linden said, his eyes twinkling as he glanced at Harper. "I can't say that I wouldn't be swayed by her either, though. She is a vision."

Jared couldn't be sure, but he was almost positive he heard Trask snort.

"I wouldn't say I'm a vision," Harper said, moving closer. "I do love Whisper Cove, though."

"Harper Harlow," Linden said, his voice taking off a faraway quality as he racked his brain. "You aren't related to Phil Harlow, are you?"

Harper sighed. "It depends," she answered. "What did he do?"

Linden chuckled. "He didn't do anything, my dear," he said. "We went to summer camp together several years in a row. I always found him delightful. He's your father, correct?"

Harper nodded. "He is my dad."

"That would make Earl Harlow your grandfather," Linden said. "I knew him through business dealings he had with my father. They worked together on a development near the shoreline a good fifty years ago. He was a wonderful man."

"He was," Harper said, an odd lump lodging in her throat. Her grandfather died more than twenty years before and she still missed him. Ironically, it was her grandfather's death that revealed she could see and talk to ghosts. He visited her after passing away and before moving on. Her parents didn't believe her at the time when she said her grandfather was there, but they did now – even though they weren't remotely interested in her job. "I miss him a lot."

"I'm sure you do," Linden said, his expression thoughtful. "Did your grandfather ever take you golfing with him?"

Harper nodded. "He did," she confirmed. "He would let me drive the cart even though I could barely reach the pedals."

"I know," Linden said. "You ran his cart into mine one day at the course in New Baltimore. You were tiny, barely up to my waist. That blond hair of yours was wild and you kept denying you drove into my cart on purpose and instead claimed a woman in an evening gown ran in front of you and caused you to swerve."

Harper stilled, surprised. She had no memory of the incident, but if she had to guess she didn't think it was a woman she saw, but a ghost. She thought her grandfather was the first ghost she encountered. Perhaps she was wrong. "I'm sorry," she said. "I don't remember that."

"You were very small and your grandfather bribed you with ice cream not to tell anyone what you did, if I remember correctly," Linden said. "You got Blue Moon and your mouth and tongue were stained for hours."

"It's weird that you two have met," Jared said.

"It's a small world," Linden agreed. "Well, we'll have to catch up later. I would love to hear how your father is doing, Ms. Harlow. Is he still as crazy as ever?"

"You have no idea," Harper said.

"Well, I have to make sure a murder goes off without a hitch. Will you excuse me?"

"Absolutely," Harper said, flashing him a smile before she shot Trask a sneer as he followed his boss out the door.

"That was interesting," Jared said once it was just the two of them. "You knew Josh's father."

"I didn't really know him," Harper argued. "My grandfather knew him."

"You were tight with your grandfather, right?"

Harper nodded. "I loved him."

"Well, maybe Linden will have some good stories for you later on," Jared said. "For now, we have to prepare ourselves for a fake murder. I don't know what to expect, but it has to be better than a real murder."

"And people say you're not smart," Harper teased.

NINE

Cameron Wilkinson's death was a thing of beauty. He was stabbed through the heart with an ornate letter opener, his body left at the foot of one of the library ladders. A pool of fake blood cascaded to the floor next to his body and Jared had to swallow his laughter when he saw the horrified look on Trask's face.

Harper and Jared watched the proceedings with unveiled interest. They positioned themselves at the far side of the room so they could hear and see everything and yet not get in the way.

The murder mystery participants took things seriously. They snapped photos with their cell phones, they looked in the dead man's pockets, and they scoured every inch of the library for clues.

It was lunchtime when they finally finished, and once Jared and Harper were the only ones left, Cameron Wilkinson climbed up from the ground with little pomp and circumstance and shot Harper a rueful smile. "It pays the bills."

"I think it looks fun," Harper said, grinning. "You made an excellent dead man."

"It's not my first time," the man said. "My real name is Hal Baker, by the way. I run the Michigan Mystery Troupe. Josh said you guys are here to observe how things go instead of participate. What do you think so far?"

"I think it looks fun and your presentation was marvelous," Harper replied.

"It looked pretty real," Jared agreed, moving closer to Hal so he could study the man's shirt. "What did you use for blood?"

"It's a mixture of corn syrup and food coloring," Hal replied. "It's sticky and gross – and I have to take a shower before lunch – but it's fairly believable."

"I'll say," Harper said, glancing closer at the letter opener. "Is that a plastic prop?"

"Nope. It's the real deal," Hal said. "It's about two centuries old. We have a number of pieces we use for this type of thing. I even have an ancient revolver. It doesn't work, but it's gorgeous to look at."

Jared took the letter opener from Hal so he could study it up close. "This thing could be legitimately dangerous if someone isn't careful," he said. "Aren't you worried one of these mystery mavens is accidentally going to flip out and stab someone?"

"Not really," Hal replied. "It's never happened before. I don't know why it would happen now. It's a prop. The people who come to these things are geeks. They're not murderers."

"Ignore him," Harper said. "He's a police officer. He sees danger around every corner."

"Maybe that's because you keep finding trouble," Jared shot back.

"I don't think you're allowed to talk to me like that after what you said to Josh this morning," Harper chided. "In fact, I'm going to expect a very long massage in the bathtub tonight if you want to get back in my good graces again."

"Oh, Heart, you had me at bath," Jared said, handing the letter opener back to Hal. "I hope you recover from your death quickly, Hal. I have to take my girl to lunch and then I think I'm going to have busy hands."

Hal chuckled. "I think you're going to have more fun than I am."

"I think you're right," Jared said.

"THE SKY is getting dark," Harper said two hours later, pointing toward the western skyline and shielding her eyes from the sun. "I think a storm is coming."

Jared followed her gaze and frowned. Instead of returning to their room after lunch Harper suggested a walk by the water. She loved the lake and wanted to wade for a little bit while they soaked up some rays and shared a few minutes alone. Jared would've preferred swimming in their tub, but he refused to be a spoilsport.

"I'll check my phone for a forecast," Jared said. "If it's going to storm, that's going to make our evening with the mystery freaks really creepy. You just know they're going to start seeing murderers behind every curtain and crouching in every shadow."

"It could be fun," Harper hedged. "Although, I was hoping to spend time on our balcony tonight. We kind of forgot about that part of the plan when we got back to our room last night."

"Yes, well … that tub is as magical as you are," Jared said. "It has the ability to distract me in the same manner you do." Jared didn't witness Harper rolling her eyes because he was focused on his phone. "I've got some bad news for you."

"I like a storm," Harper volunteered. "It will cut into our balcony plans, but there's nothing I love more than a good thunderstorm to cuddle my way through."

"You're definitely going to get that," Jared said. "I think you might get more than that, though. According to this we're supposed to get almost two full days of storms. They're supposed to keep rolling in one after the other."

"It's the heat and humidity," Harper said. "That always happens during the summer months. It's especially bad close to the water."

"I guess that means we're going to be doing a lot of cuddling," Jared said, winking at Harper. "I think I'm up for it, but I might need some motivation." He suggestively tapped his cheek and Harper rolled up to the balls of her feet and planted a kiss on him.

"Are you happy?" she asked.

"I'm getting there," Jared said, shoving his phone back in his pocket. "I think the storm is still two hours away."

"Not according to those clouds," Harper said.

"We'll watch them and see," Jared said. "We'll have plenty of time to get back to the hotel if it gets darker. For now, you can enjoy your wading."

Harper smirked as she turned back to the water. She'd been dying to ask Jared a question since his conversation with Linden earlier in the day, but now she wasn't sure if she should.

She watched as Jared sidled up beside her and dipped his toes into the water.

"That's cold," he said.

"It's refreshing."

"I think you might secretly be an Eskimo," Jared said, kicking his toes through the water. He leaned over when something caught his eye and rummaged through the sand with his hand until he came up with a gold necklace. It glinted beneath the sun and Jared studied it with impassioned eyes.

"What's that?" Harper asked.

"It's a necklace," Jared said, trying to open the hinged heart. "It's a locket."

"Don't do that," Harper said. "You might break it. You should give it to someone at the hotel and see if anyone lost it."

"That's a good idea," Jared said, shoving the locket into his pocket. "It's probably old or something, but it can't hurt to ask."

"Hmm," Harper said, returning to her previous thoughts.

"What are you thinking?" Jared asked.

Harper swiveled quickly and plastered an innocent look on her face. "I'm not thinking about anything but how nice the water feels."

"Don't lie," Jared chided. "You're bad at it and I can tell when you're thinking about something. Is it the nightmare you had last night?"

Harper scowled. "No," she said. "You need to let that go. Although … I don't really want to encourage you, but I remembered something else about my dream."

"What's that?"

"I had red hair," Harper said. "It was a lot longer than my normal hair and it was red and wavy. Well, actually it was more of a blondish red. I think Zander would refer to it as auburn."

"Okay," Jared said. "Why is that important?"

"I don't think I was dreaming about myself," Harper explained. "I think I was dreaming about someone else."

"Who?"

Harper shrugged. "I honestly have no idea," she said. "I probably have murder on the brain because we're at a murder mystery event. The only reason I'm even telling you what I remembered is because I know you're worried I'm going to freak out because of what happened with Jim."

"I'm not worried you're going to freak out," Jared clarified. "I want you to know that I'm here if you need to talk and I don't like it when you have nightmares. There's a difference. I think all of your dreams should be full of nudity, sex, and me."

"Ah, well, I'll get right on that," Harper deadpanned, trilling as she splashed through the water. "Do you know what we should do when we get home?"

"Hammock?"

Harper chuckled. "I keep telling you that hammock isn't a verb," she said. "I'm glad you enjoyed our afternoon hammocking, though. I did, too."

"I definitely want to do that again," Jared said. "It's too bad we couldn't find a way to put a hammock in that bathtub. Then we'd really have the best of both worlds. We'd be happy forever and never leave."

"I think snow would force us to leave but … ." Harper broke off, biting her lower lip. The question she so desperately wanted to ask niggled the back of her brain again.

"Tell me what's on your mind, Harper," Jared instructed. "I can see you thinking and whatever it is you're worrying about is big enough that you practically have smoke coming out of your ears."

"That's a gross exaggeration."

"I learned it from Zander," Jared said. "Talk."

Harper sighed, resigned. "It's something you said to Linden," she admitted. "I didn't want to ask you about it in front of him – and if you weren't serious and just making conversation I totally understand – but I want to know if you meant what you said."

Jared was puzzled. "About what?"

"Do you really think you'll stay in Whisper Cove?"

"Oh, *that*," Jared said, his expression softening. "I should've realized you were thinking about that. I know I've been thinking about it a lot lately."

"And?"

"I can't make you any promises, but ... I like Whisper Cove," Jared said. "There are possibilities for me to stay with the local department full-time and still be tasked with the sheriff's department on certain jobs. That holds some appeal."

"But?" Harper prodded.

"But I always fancied myself walking gritty streets and solving big crimes every day," Jared admitted. "That was my dream from when I was a little boy. Now? Well, now I have a new dream. I don't know how to handle that, though."

"What's your new dream?"

"I think you're fishing for compliments," Jared teased, wagging a finger.

"I honestly wasn't," Harper said. "I want to know what you want."

"Harper, we haven't been dating for very long yet," Jared cautioned. "I like you a lot, but we can't make a plan for that far down the road. You know that, right?"

Harper made a "well, duh" face and rolled her eyes. "I'm not asking you to commit to me forever," she said. "I'm asking if you would really consider staying in Whisper Cove. I thought you would always move on to a bigger department."

"Are you worried that means I'm going to automatically move on from you?" Jared asked.

"I ... ." Harper didn't know how to answer. "I guess I would be lying if I said it had never crossed my mind. I brought it up to Zander and he said you would probably be moving to a job that wasn't too far away so it wouldn't really matter."

"Well, Zander is right," Jared said. "Whether or not I decide to leave the Whisper Cove Police Department it will have nothing to do with our relationship. I happen to be pretty happy. I hope we're still happy when it comes time to make a decision. Neither one of us can see the future, though. We'll have to tough it out."

"Tough it out?"

"Hey, all of these baths are torture," Jared said, smiling as he reached for Harper so he could offer her a reassuring hug. "Someone has to do it. I'm taking one for the team."

"You're such a hero," Harper said, laughing as Jared lifted her off the ground and swung her around.

After a few moments of cavorting, Jared lowered Harper, but he didn't let her go. "If I decide to get another job, you'll be a part of that decision," he said. "Don't worry that I'm going to change my mind on the spur of the moment and walk away from you. That's not in me."

"Because you're a good guy," Harper supplied, nodding as she pressed her lips together.

"Because I can't get enough of you," Jared corrected. "I don't want to be away from you one second longer than I have to be. That's not one day. That's every single day. Sure, some of that can be attributed to the heady early days of a new relationship, but I'm pretty sure I'm going to want to be around you for a good long while."

"Even if I make fun of your nipples?"

"Even if," Jared said, tracing the line of her angular jaw. "You make me happy. I hope I make you happy."

"I haven't been this happy in a really long time," Harper said.

"Good." Jared lowered his mouth and planted a hot kiss on Harper, dragging her as close as he could without absorbing her inside of him. They were lost in the moment, the outside world disappearing, and then someone cleared their throat a few feet away.

Jared shifted his eyes to the garden path and found Josh watching them with an impish grin. "What do you want?"

"Am I interrupting something?" Josh asked, feigning innocence.

"You have the worst timing ever," Jared said.

"I know," Josh said, his smile slipping. "I know you're not going to like this, but I need a favor."

"Oh, well, great," Jared muttered. "I can already tell this is going to suck."

TEN

"Why would I do you a favor after you interrupted me and my girl?" Jared asked, keeping his arm around Harper's waist as he regarded Josh. "Seriously, I was in a happy, happy place."

"I saw that," Josh said. "I waited as long as I could. You guys appeared to be having a deep discussion. Then you swung her around like a high school jock celebrating a touchdown. Then you started making out.

"I was afraid it was going to go further so I had to interrupt you," he continued. "I'm truly sorry ... mostly because I was hoping for nudity."

"You're such a pig," Jared snapped.

"That's because you encourage him," Harper said. "What's going on, Josh? Is something wrong?"

"Yes and no," Josh replied, tugging a restless hand through his hair. "Did you see the weather report?"

"We noticed the sky," Jared said, pointing. "The Weather Channel app says the storm is still two hours away but that when it gets here it's going to be a two-day soaker."

"It's technically three different storm systems," Josh said. "It will have the same outcome, though."

"You always have to be right, don't you?"

"Look who's talking," Josh shot back. "I really did come down here for a reason – other than spying on you and Harper, that is."

"What's the reason?" Jared asked.

"We have a shipment of wine sitting at the dock in New Baltimore," Josh replied. "It's supposed to come over with tomorrow's ferry because we can't spare someone to pick it up, but if the storm is too bad, there won't be a ferry."

"Oh," Jared said, realization dawning. "You want me to pick it up, don't you?"

"I know it's a lot to ask when you're on vacation with the prettiest girl in the world, but I'm pretty much desperate," Josh said. "We're not going to run out of wine tonight, but if the storm does hang on and is as brutal as they say, the ferry won't be running and we're going to run out of wine tomorrow."

"What's the big deal?" Harper questioned. "You have plenty of other liquor. Can't they drink something else?"

"I don't know if you saw that display at the body discovery this morning, but these are not normal people," Josh said. "Don't get me wrong, I think they're funny and endearing. I've never seen anything like that in my life, though. They took their investigation very seriously.

"Now, if they take a fake investigation that seriously, what's going to happen if I run out of red wine?" he asked.

"That's a very good point," Jared said, shifting his eyes to Harper. "Can I make it to New Baltimore and back before the storm hits?"

"It shouldn't be a problem," Josh said. "You're going to have to leave now, though."

"Okay." Jared moved to walk up the pathway, but Harper grabbed his hand. "What?"

"I'll come with you."

"No, you stay here," Jared said. "The roads might be dodgy and you're a distraction when the weather is perfect. Besides, I brought my truck. I need to put the crate somewhere so it doesn't get wet and the easiest place is in the passenger seat."

"I didn't think of that," Harper said. "What if you get lost, though? You don't know the area very well."

"It's right at the dock, Harper," Josh supplied. "He'll pull off the ferry, stop at the first building, show the worker the order form I'm going to give him and then pull right back onto the ferry. He shouldn't be gone more than an hour."

"I still think I should go," Harper pressed.

"I think you're cute when you worry, but you should stay here," Jared said. "You're not going to have a lot of time to splash around in the lake. Take the next hour and have your fun, because the only place you're going to be splashing after that is that tub."

Harper tried to rein in her smile, but she couldn't muster the energy. "Do you promise to be careful?"

"I promise," Jared said, leaning forward so he could give her a soft kiss. "You probably won't even miss me."

"I don't think that's true," Harper said. "Be careful, though. Take your time driving back. Don't rush on my account."

"You're the only reason I would rush, Heart," Jared said, tugging on a strand of her hair. "I'll be back before you know it."

"DO you want me to stay out here with you?" Josh asked Harper twenty minutes later, glancing at the darkening sky. "I think the storm is going to get here before the weather forecasters predicted."

"Jared won't get stuck in New Baltimore, will he?" Harper asked. "I mean ... he'll get back to this side without a problem, right?"

"It's rush hour, Harper," Josh said. "People are coming home from work. If the ferry didn't transport people, the officials who run the service would never hear the end of it. I promise he'll come back."

"I hope so," Harper said, her tone reflecting worry instead of hope. "You don't have to wait for me. I'm going to spend five more minutes looking around and then head back."

"Are you sure?" Josh pressed. "I can wait and walk you back if you're afraid of being out here alone."

"You seem to forget I run ghost tours and scare people for a living," Harper said. "I don't scare easily. I'll be fine."

"I know," Josh said, unmoved by Harper's blasé attitude. "Jared wouldn't forgive me if something happened to you, though."

"What's going to happen to me?"

"I don't know," Josh said. "What if you fall in the lake and drown?"

"I promise to put my shoes on without dallying and head up," Harper said, giving in just as the wind started whipping itself into a frenzy. "You need to go up now, though. Your guests are probably worried and they're going to need someone to corral them.

"In fact, if you've hidden clues outside for the game, you might want to collect them now," she continued. "If you don't, I think you're going to lose them."

"That's a very good point," Josh said. "You've got fifteen minutes to get your cute little behind up to the hotel. If I don't see you there in that time, I'm sending out a search party and tattling to Jared when he gets back."

"That's not a very adult thing to do."

"Yes, well, Jared is going to kill me if something happens to you," Josh replied. "I would rather tattle on you than lose my life. Be quick about this. I honestly think this storm is going to be a doozy."

"I'm kind of excited," Harper said. "I love a good storm."

"Then I think you're in for a treat."

JARED WAS WORRIED. THE FERRY OFFICIALS USHERED HIM ONTO the platform without hesitation, but the tug didn't leave on time. Finally, Jared couldn't take not knowing what was going on so he approached the officials. They had their heads bent together as they studied the choppy waves.

"What's going on?" Jared asked. "Why aren't we moving?"

"A storm is coming," one of the men said. "It's going to be a big one."

"I noticed that," Jared said. "We have time to get to the island, though. If you wait much longer, we might not make it."

"We're trying to get as many commuters on the ferry as possible," the man said. "Whatever happens, this is going to be the last ferry. Once this tug pulls away, everyone on that island is stuck there for tonight – possibly tomorrow, too – and everyone on this side is going to be separated from their loved ones if they need to get over there."

Harper's face floated into Jared's field of vision. "I need to get over there and I'm scared that you're not going to leave when it's time. We should leave now."

"I've been doing this fifteen years," the man said. "We can wait fifteen minutes."

Jared was frustrated. "If I don't get back over there my girlfriend is going to be stranded alone."

"Do you think you're the only one with that problem?"

"No," Jared said. "I do think I need to get over there, though."

"Son, we're doing the best we can," the man said. "Get back in your vehicle. The rain is almost here. We'll leave as soon as humanly possible."

Jared could only hope that was true. If he was separated from Harper because of this storm, he was definitely going to beat up Josh.

"WHAT IS THAT NOISE?" ZANDER ASKED, SCREECHING THROUGH the phone as Harper pressed it to her ear during the walk back to the Stokes Hotel. "It sounds like you're in a tornado."

"You're not far off," Harper said. "There's a huge storm heading this way. You're safe, right?"

"I'm fine, Harp," Zander said. She could practically see him rolling his eyes through the phone. "Storms always hit worse on the water than they do on land. Where are you?"

"Walking back to the hotel."

"In the middle of a storm?"

"It's not storming yet," Harper replied. "It will be soon, though. Jared had to go to New Baltimore to pick up a case of wine so we don't run out and I'm really worried he's not going to make it back before they shut down the ferry."

"It's going to be okay, Harp," Zander said. "Even if Jared does get stranded, you have your own room and you're at a fake murder event. It's not a real one so there's no reason to get worked up."

"I'm not worked up."

"You sound worked up."

"I might be a little worked up," Harper conceded after a beat. "It's not about the storm, though."

"Okay, I'll bite," Zander said. "What's troubling you?"

"Jared told his friend's father that he's considering staying in Whisper Cove no matter what now." Zander was so quiet on the other end of the phone Harper worried she'd lost him. "Zander?"

"I'm here," Zander said, recovering quickly. "How do you feel about that? Are you happy?"

"I'm … torn," Harper said. "On one hand, if he stays in Whisper Cove we'll be close to one another all the time. I like that. On the other, he's always dreamed about being a cop in a grittier city."

"Even if he takes a job in Detroit or Warren, he'll still be able to commute to Whisper Cove," Zander pointed out. "It's not the end of the world."

"He said that, too," Harper acknowledged. "The other part that worries me is that he would be safer in Whisper Cove. The past few months notwithstanding, our crime is generally a lot less violent. I don't want to worry about him not coming home."

"Because Quinn never came home," Zander supplied, referring to Harper's former boyfriend who disappeared after a car accident and was presumed dead. She searched for his ghost for months, convinced he was wandering the countryside looking for peace. She never found him. The police said he lost too much blood and the injuries he sustained would've been catastrophic. She knew he was dead. She still worried his spirit was out there.

"I know it's wrong to say because Quinn was a good guy, but I never cared about him the same way I care about Jared," Harper said. "It's early, but … I like him."

"I know you like him," Zander said dryly. "Trust me. The whole town knows you like him. He likes you, too. It would be great if he stayed in Whisper Cove. That's what you want. Why are you worried about this?"

"Because I'm afraid it's not what he really wants and he'll end up resenting me if he stays and misses out on his chance to do something bigger," Harper said.

"Harp, I … ." Zander didn't get a chance to finish his statement because Harper lost her signal at the same moment a huge bolt of lightning landed in the field across the road from the hotel.

Harper's eyebrows flew up as she scanned the area, her heart rolling when she saw a figure standing close to the edge of the road. Harper moved in that direction without thinking things through and she was almost on top of the woman before she realized she could see through her.

"Oh, crap," Harper muttered, staring the ghost down. Up close she was pretty – beautiful even. She had long auburn hair and sad blue eyes. "Are you lost?"

The ghost didn't respond.

"I can't stay out here," Harper said. "The storm is almost here. I'll come back to help you when it passes. I promise. Where will you be?"

The ghost didn't speak. Instead she pointed in the direction of the cemetery and Harper shot her a wry smile.

"Of course. You're in the cemetery."

A terrific roar of thunder washed over Harper, echoing against the water as the waves beat against the shoreline's rocky coast.

"I have to go," Harper said, taking a step back. "I'm sorry. I'll come back. It's not safe out here. You're already dead so that's not an issue. I will be dead if I don't get inside right now. I … ." Harper jolted when another rumble of thunder shook the ground. "I have to go."

Harper was ready to run when she swiveled, pulling up short when she saw Josh standing behind her. "You scared the crap out of me," she hissed, slapping his arm. "That was not funny. What are you doing out here?"

"Looking for you!"

"Oh."

"Who were you talking to?" Josh asked, his eyes busy as they focused on the empty spot the ghost stood moments before.

"Um … myself?" Harper had no idea how to answer.

"I think you and I need to have a talk."

ELEVEN

"**D**o you want to tell me what just happened?"

Josh pulled Harper into a small sitting room located off the foyer and closed the door so prying ears couldn't hear their conversation.

"I don't know what you're talking about," Harper said, forcing her gaze to remain level as she faced off with Josh. "The storm is almost here. We should really check and make sure all the guests are back inside and not wandering around or lost."

"That's what the staff is for," Josh said, cutting Harper off so she didn't have an easy path to the door. "Who were you talking to?"

"What makes you think I was talking to anyone?"

"Your lips were moving and I heard you," Josh said. "You said you had to go but you would find whoever you were talking to later so you could help them. Who were you talking to?"

"I was talking to myself."

Josh narrowed his eyes as he looked Harper up and down. Her hair was a mess, the wind whipping it into a mass of loose waves, and she looked defiant. "I don't believe you."

"I don't know what you want me to do with that," Harper said, opting for honesty. "I'm sorry you don't believe me, but no one was out there. You saw that for yourself. I talk to myself all of the time. It's stupid and embarrassing to be caught, but … there it is."

"Harper, if something is going on … ."

"Nothing is going on," Harper said, cutting him off. "I don't understand why you're so bothered by this. People talk to themselves all of the time."

"Does Jared know you walk around talking to yourself all of the time?" Josh pressed.

"I don't know," Harper replied stiffly. "Perhaps you should ask him."

"I might just do that."

HARPER MADE A SHOW OF CHECKING ON GUESTS FOR THE NEXT hour, but she was really hiding from Josh. She had no idea what to do. She could've followed Jared's advice and admitted her secret, but she didn't feel comfortable baring her soul to a man she'd just met. Of course, she bared her soul to Jared not long after meeting him and that turned out fine. Jared was different, though. He was … special.

The ghost by the road was another problem. Harper was used to lonely souls popping up in strange places. Most of the time they kept to themselves and didn't hurt anyone. She only heard about pesky ghosts, like Archibald. The quiet ones … the tortured ones … they were a different story.

On a whim, Harper made her way to the library and searched it for wandering guests before pulling her phone out of her pocket. She faced the door so she could see anyone entering and almost cried out in relief when Zander answered.

"You scared me to death, Harp," Zander snapped. "What happened?"

"The storm hit," Harper answered, briefly shifting her eyes to the window where the rain splattered in a horizontal pattern. "I'm okay. I didn't even get wet."

"Is Jared back yet?"

"No," Harper replied. "Something else happened, though, and I'm freaking out."

"Oh, good, a crisis," Zander intoned. "I thought I was going to be stuck in this house alone for the next two days with nothing to do but watch the rain. If you're having a meltdown, though, that means I won't be bored."

"Ha, ha."

"Your father stopped in to make sure we had a storm safety kit, by the way," Zander said. "He says it's never too late to start leading a responsible life and then he handed me a flashlight and a can of SpaghettiOs."

Harper snorted. "He's probably just lonely," she said. "A storm is going to cut down on his dating options. He can't crawl out of bathroom windows in the middle of a potential tornado and expect not to get caught."

Harper's parents were mired in the world's most tempestuous divorce. She spent her younger years expecting a divorce. She spent her teenage years fervently wishing for one. By the time she hit adulthood she figured Phil and Gloria Harlow could survive anything. That's why their divorce announcement came as such a shock.

Now, just like when they were pretending to be happily married, Phil and Gloria insisted on fighting about everything. Their divorce was nowhere near being settled because they spent weeks arguing about who got the toner cartridges for the printer, amongst a myriad of other petty grievances. The most recent fight was about a pair of salt and pepper shakers from Disney World.

"Do you know who won the salt and pepper shakers?" Harper asked.

"They're still haggling," Zander replied. "I suggested splitting them up so your father could have Mickey and your mother could have Minnie, but that didn't go over well."

"You should know better," Harper said, relaxing despite herself. Zander always knew how to make her feel better, even when things were spiraling out of control and her boyfriend was missing in a storm. "Josh heard me talking to a ghost."

Zander was silent on the other end of the phone. It unnerved Harper. He was never silent ... well, unless his mouth was full of food.

"Zander?"

"I heard you," Zander said. "I'm trying to decide how to answer. Why don't we start with the ghost? Where did you see him?"

"It's a her," Harper replied. "She was standing by the road when I came back to the hotel. In fact, a huge bolt of lightning struck in the field across the way and that's what drew my attention to her. I thought she was in trouble and didn't realize she was a ghost until I was right on top of her."

"Did she speak to you?"

"The storm was really ramping up and I told her I had to go and would find her later," Harper explained. "I asked where she would be and she pointed toward the cemetery."

"I forgot that place has its own cemetery," Zander said. "That was always a cool place."

"Josh is looking for ideas for theme weekends and I gave him a few, including a gay spa weekend for you and a haunted murder mystery for me," Harper said. "He was excited at the time, but now he thinks I'm crazy."

"Who do you think the ghost is?" Zander asked, all pretense of messing around gone. "Do you think she's recent?"

Harper searched her memory regarding her brief encounter with the spirit. "Her clothes were dated," Harper said. "I would guess they were at least twenty years old – maybe longer."

"They weren't eighties clothes, were they?" Zander asked, horrified. "Imagine dying a horrible death and being stuck in a 'Freddy says Relax' shirt with Day-Glo shoelaces for the duration of your afterlife."

Harper giggled at the visual. "You always know how to make me feel better."

"That's my job."

"No, she wasn't wearing eighties clothing," Harper said. "I think she was wearing shoulder pads, though."

"Ugh, that's just as bad," Zander said. "Was she wearing one of those silk button-down tops, too? You know the eighties hung around well into the nineties for some people in this area."

"It didn't look like a silk shirt, but it was ugly," Harper replied. "She was youngish. I would say she was in her mid-thirties at the most, although I can't be sure because I had absolutely no time to get a good read on her."

"And what happened?" Zander prodded. "Josh came up on you when you were talking to her, is that it?"

"I turned around to run to the hotel and he was standing there," Harper said. "He asked me who I was talking to and I told him I was talking to myself. He didn't believe me and hauled me into a little room to question me when we got back, but I stuck to my story."

"I'm not sure that talking to yourself doesn't make you crazier than admitting you were talking to a ghost," Zander said. "How did Josh seem?"

"Bothered."

"Do you want to expand on that?"

"He just kept pestering me about who I was talking to and then he asked if Jared knew I talked to myself," Harper said. "I told him he would have to ask Jared and he said he planned to do just that."

"Well, it could be worse," Zander mused. "You should've said you were talking to me. You could've said we were talking and you lost me because of the lightning strike and were trying to get me back on speakerphone."

"I didn't think of that."

"Well, it's too late now," Zander said. "I wouldn't worry about it, Harp. Jared knows you weren't talking to yourself and when Josh approaches him he'll understand what happened and brush it off. It's not a big deal."

"It feels like a big deal."

"That's because you're naturally dramatic and pessimistic," Zander said. "You're at a murder mystery event with a storm bearing down. You talking to yourself is going to be the farthest thing from Josh's mind once he realizes everything else he has to deal with."

"What happens if Jared doesn't make it back?"

"He'll make it back," Zander said. "He'll show up on that island no matter what, even if he has to swim."

"That doesn't make me feel better."

"It's going to be okay, Harp," Zander soothed. "Just think, though, if Jared does get stranded on this side of the water, he'll probably come here and I'll have to entertain him all night. We can compare nipples."

"I love you, Zander," Harper said.

"I love you, too."

AFTER ANOTHER FIVE MINUTES OF PACING IN THE LIBRARY, Harper made her way back to the foyer. The guests seemed unperturbed by the storm – some were even excited for the shift in ambiance – and the staff was working overtime to keep them happy.

Harper positioned herself by the far wall so she could watch the front door. She was desperate for word from Jared. She'd tried calling him three times, but she kept getting his voicemail. She knew that didn't necessarily mean anything – especially if he was on the ferry and not getting proper cell service – but she was uneasy.

"I'm sure Jared will be back soon," Linden said, appearing at Harper's side. "Josh told me he sent Jared to pick up the wine. I'm thankful he went, but I'm sorry you're so worried."

"I'm not worried," Harper said, putting on a brave face. "Jared is very capable. He's probably taking his time coming back just to be safe."

"You don't have to put on an act for me," Linden said. "I can see your worry. Jared has always been a solid friend for Josh. He's stalwart and strong. I'm glad he's in the area. I'm hoping he'll be a good influence on Josh."

Harper stilled. "I thought Josh was running everything," she said. "I was under the impression he was doing a good job."

"He's doing a tremendous job given the circumstances," Linden said. "He's got grand plans and I hope they work. He still needs someone to center him so he doesn't fly off into the sky like a balloon. Jared is good like that."

"Jared is good at everything he does," Harper said. "He seems to really like Josh. I'm glad he has a friend in the area, too. I worry he gets bored hanging out with Zander and me all of the time."

"And Zander is the man you live with?"

"I see Josh has been telling you all about me," Harper said. "Yes, though. Zander is my best friend. We've never been romantically involved, though."

"I understand," Linden said. "Josh told me about the arrangement. He thought it was funny, I find it intriguing. He says Jared is very happy with you."

"I hope so."

"I wouldn't worry about that, my dear," Linden said. "Jared seems almost blissful from what I've been able to ascertain. You're obviously a big part of that."

"Thank you."

"I'm sure Jared will be back soon," Linden said, patting Harper's arm. "Don't fret. If you're bored, though, they're about to discover another body in the arboretum."

Harper smirked. "That sounds fun."

"Yes, everyone enjoys finding a body," Linden said. "I find I've been entertained throughout this entire thing, despite my initial misgivings. I really must go and oversee the next event, though. If you get worried, you can seek me out."

"I'm okay," Harper said, forcing a smile. "Thank you for checking on me."

"Of course," Linden said. "I know your family and I'm fond of your boyfriend. You're practically a member of my family yourself. If you need anything, don't hesitate to ask. That's what the staff is here for."

"Thank you."

Harper watched Linden go, shifting her eyes to Josh once his father left the room. Josh's expression was hard to read as he talked to a middle-aged woman close to the bar area. She seemed to be engaged in a wild story and Josh was doing his best to appear interested. It was obvious his mind was someplace else, though. Harper knew it was on her, and she had no idea how to handle it.

Three bright flashes of lightning flashed outside the window, causing the power to dim and then fail. The room plunged into darkness and everyone – guests and staff alike – started murmuring amongst themselves.

"Don't worry," Josh called out. "We have a generator. It will kick on in thirty seconds. Nothing bad will happen in that time. I promise you won't miss anything."

As if on cue the front door opened at the exact moment a rumble of thunder rolled over the area. It was strong enough to shake the floor. The guests screamed and gasped, and Harper pushed herself away from the door and launched herself on Jared as soon as she recognized him.

"I was so worried!"

TWELVE

"I'm glad to see you missed me," Jared said, chuckling as he wrapped his arms around Harper. "I missed you, too."

"I was so worried," Harper said, her voice shaking. "I honestly didn't think you were going to make it back and I didn't want to stay here alone."

Jared rubbed Harper's back, keeping her close as he shut the door. When the lights flashed back on, he pulled back far enough that he could search her face for clues as to what was bothering her. "What's wrong?"

"Nothing," Harper replied hurriedly. "I'm fine. I was just worried about you."

"I don't think that's all that's wrong," Jared prodded. "Do you want to tell me about it?"

Harper furtively glanced around. "Not here."

"Okay," Jared said, taking her answer in stride. "We can talk upstairs. I have to change. I'm soaking wet … and now you are, too."

"I'm so glad you made it," Harper said, throwing her arms around his neck again, paying no heed to the fact that she was drenching her own outfit.

"I would've found a way to get to you no matter what," Jared said,

LILY HARPER HART

kissing her cheek. He was worried. Something had clearly happened during his absence. "Let's go upstairs."

Harper wordlessly nodded and cringed when she turned to find Josh approaching. "Great."

Jared knit his eyebrows together but otherwise remained expressionless. "Your wine is on the front seat of my truck. You're going to have to send someone else out to get it because I'm not going back out in that."

"That's fine," Josh said, smiling. "I'm glad you made it. I think Harper was starting to get worried."

"I noticed that," Jared said, rubbing his thumb across the back of Harper's neck. "This is what happens when you're manly and save the night's wine supply."

"I guess so," Josh said. "I was starting to get worried about her. Then I found her talking to herself by the road right before the storm hit. I was definitely worried then."

"Talking to herself?" Jared glanced at Harper.

"She said she does it all the time and that you knew about it and nothing was going on," Josh said.

Harper's warm feelings regarding the man were fading fast in light of his tattletale nature. "We should get you out of those clothes, Jared."

Jared ignored the suggestion. "I don't think there's anything wrong with talking to yourself," he said. "I do it all the time."

"Yes, but she was talking about having to leave because of the storm but helping someone once the weather got better," Josh said. "It didn't sound like she was talking to herself."

"I don't think it matters," Jared replied, unruffled. "Was she hurting anyone?"

"No," Josh said, shifting uncomfortably from one foot to the other. "It was just … odd."

"I don't see what's odd about it, but if you're upset I guess she can keep her conversations with herself to … well … herself, if that makes you feel better."

"I didn't mean to upset anyone, least of all Harper," Josh said. "I just … was worried about her."

"You don't need to worry about her," Jared said, squeezing Harp-

88

er's hand. "She can take care of herself. I'm here to take care of her now, though. Don't worry about a thing. Everything is under control."

"I ... ." Josh closed his mouth and nodded. "I'm sorry."

"Don't be," Jared said. "Everything is fine."

"EVERYTHING IS NOT FINE," HARPER PRACTICALLY EXPLODED the second Jared closed their suite door five minutes later. "He thinks I'm crazy."

"You *are* crazy," Jared said. "What were you doing talking to a ghost in the middle of a dangerous storm?"

"How do you know what I was doing?" Harper asked.

"Because I'm not an idiot," Jared replied, tugging his shirt off and dropping it on the floor. "You don't generally walk around talking to yourself unless Zander has caused you to flip your lid."

"Oh."

"Oh," Jared said, nodding knowingly. "Come here."

"What? Why?"

"Come here," Jared repeated, his temper wearing thin.

Harper took an uncertain step toward him and then willingly stepped into his embrace when he opened his arms. "I'm sorry I ruined this trip," she murmured into his shoulder. "Your friend thinks I'm crazy and I ruined everything."

"You haven't ruined anything," Jared countered. "This is why I didn't want to hide your abilities. You shouldn't be ashamed of them. You're amazing."

"I didn't know he was behind me," Harper said. "I didn't realize I was walking toward a ghost until I was almost on top of her. I thought she was a regular woman and she might need help. The storm was almost on us and ... I'm so sorry."

"Knock it off, Heart," Jared said, swaying as he rubbed her back. "You have nothing to apologize for. Josh is the one who should feel like an ass. You weren't doing anything wrong."

"It didn't help that I was convinced you were going to be stranded on the other side of the lake," Harper said. "I was on the phone with

Zander and he said he was going to make you spend the night with him so you could compare nipples."

"If Zander doesn't stop talking about nipples I'm going to cut his off," Jared groused. "Everything is okay. I'm here. You're here. We're together. This place has a generator so we're not going to lose power."

Harper let him soothe her for a few minutes and then finally felt calm enough to step away. "I really was worried."

"I was worried, too," Jared conceded. "That ferry ride back over here was choppy and uncomfortable. I made it, though. We're stuck here for the next two days. I heard the ferry operators talking and they were shutting it down after the last ride. We're together, though.

"We've got a bathtub, shower, wine, and food," he continued. "What more do you want?"

"We have a ghost, too," Harper reminded him.

"Do you know anything about her?"

Harper bit her lip and shook her head. "She didn't speak."

"Well, until you know something about her, we can't do anything," Jared said. "Now that she knows you can see her, she might show up. I'll protect you if that happens and you'll be able to talk to her without fear of discovery."

"You really are wonderful."

"I know," Jared said, grinning. "That's why you're going to reward me with a shower. You're already wet so you need to get cleaned up and I need some comfort after my ordeal."

Harper snorted. "You're incorrigible."

"Come on," Jared prodded. "I'm a hero for retrieving the wine. I deserve a hero's welcome."

"Well, who am I to argue with a hero?"

"THIS SMELLS AMAZING," JARED SAID AN HOUR LATER, LEANING closer to his plate and inhaling the pasta dish. "This is exactly what I need after my death-defying trip."

Harper arched a dubious eyebrow. "Seriously? Now you almost died?"

"Yes, and you're going to have to reward me for that when we get back to our room tonight," Jared said.

"You're lucky I was really worried about you because otherwise this would not fly," Harper said, although she wasn't particularly irked. She found Jared's whims adorable. "I forgot they had another fake body discovery this afternoon. Do we know if it went well?"

"It went fine," Josh answered, taking the spot next to Harper at their table and offering her a rueful smile. "I'm sorry you guys missed it. It was my fault and I feel terrible."

"Don't worry about it," Jared said. "The drive wasn't bad and the only harrowing part was the ferry ride back. I wouldn't want to do it again, but everything turned out fine. Did you get the wine out of my truck?"

"We did and thank you."

"No problem," Jared said. "This food looks amazing, by the way."

"We're having surf and turf tomorrow, and that's really going to be amazing," Josh said. "I hope you like lobster tails because we have a lot of them and you can have as many as you want."

"Sold," Jared said, grinning at Harper. "I absolutely love seafood."

"You like all food," Harper said, although she returned his smile. "That does sound good. This looks amazing, too, though " She averted her eyes so she couldn't meet Josh's earnest stare.

"Harper, I want to apologize for earlier," Josh said. "I was out of line and I didn't mean to embarrass you."

"It's fine," Harper said, waving him off and remaining fixated on her plate. "It's honestly not a big deal."

"I don't think that's true," Josh said. "You're upset. I can see it on your face … even though you won't look me in the eye. The last thing I want to do is make you uncomfortable."

Harper pointedly locked gazes with Josh. "It's fine."

"Let it go, Josh," Jared prodded. "She's embarrassed and you're getting pathetic about making amends. Let's call a truce and move on. It's over and done with."

"Okay," Josh said.

Harper sent Josh a legitimate smile. "It really is okay," she said. "I was flustered because I lost Zander when we were talking on the phone and you scared me because I didn't hear you coming up behind me. It's not a big deal."

"As long as you're okay, I'm happy," Josh said. "I'm never going to be able to steal you away from Jared if you hate me."

"I don't hate you," Harper said, allowing herself to marginally relax.

"And he can't steal you away from me because I am the ultimate man," Jared added.

"And that, too," Harper said, giggling at Jared's mock outrage.

"Speaking of the storm, it's bound to get loud tonight," Josh said, changing the conversational topic to something less risky. "The guests are still buzzing about the death this afternoon. It was a maid, if you're interested. They'll be searching for clues all night and there might be another surprise, although I'm not allowed to broadcast the specifics. I'm actually glad about everything ramping up in the game because that will keep everyone distracted and busy."

"What do you want us to do?" Jared asked. "And when you answer, make sure you realize we're going to bed early because I need to be treated like a hero after my epic trip this afternoon."

"You're a freaking drama queen, man," Josh said, rolling his eyes. "Just watch everyone and see if they're having a good time. Tell me if any of the staff isn't playing the game correctly."

"I can guarantee your butler Trask isn't going to play," Jared said. "He gave us an earful this afternoon about how turning the house into a hotel was undignified."

"He's ... set in his ways," Josh said. "I like Trask. He's been around since I was a kid. He's never been particularly nice to me, but it's not like he was mean to me either. If I had my druthers my father would force him to toe the line.

"They've got a unique relationship, though, and my dad doesn't like bossing Trask around for some reason," he continued. "Trask basically gets to do whatever he feels like doing. If you see him being obnoxious, tell me. Otherwise just ignore him. That's what I do."

"What is his deal?" Harper asked. "Is he upset because the house isn't Downton Abbey any longer?"

Josh snickered. "Pretty much, and that's an absolutely apt way of putting it. He thinks the house is a status symbol. It's just a house, though, and if we want to keep it in the family we have to change with the times. He needs to understand it and accept it."

"Did you know your dad knows Harper's father?" Jared asked. "I guess they went to camp together as kids."

"I didn't know that," Josh said, shaking his head. "It's a small world. It's also another reason she should dump you and choose me. Our fathers already like each other."

"I'll have you know that her father adores me," Jared argued.

"Is that so?" Josh didn't look convinced.

"I believe his exact words upon meeting me were 'I guess you'll do.'"

"Well, if that's not a ringing endorsement, I don't know what is," Josh said, laughing heartily. "Now I want to meet Harper's father and her best friend. Whisper Cove sounds like a happening place."

"You have no idea," Jared said.

THIRTEEN

"**I** need to walk off this food, and we can't go outside to do it," Harper lamented after dinner, leaning back in her chair and patting her stomach. "I'm glad we didn't have to dress up tonight because there's no way I would've fit into a dress."

"You're beautiful and you know it," Jared said. "I'm stuffed, too. I know better than to eat that much and yet I can't seem to stop myself."

"You're a glutton."

"Pretty much," Jared agreed.

"Maybe we should take a walk down some of these hallways before whatever tonight's big murder mystery event happens to be goes down," Harper suggested.

"We can do that," Jared said, balling up his napkin and dropping it on the table. "Let's take a walk."

Jared let Harper pick the direction as they left the dining room and he wasn't surprised she opted for the hallway that led past the library. Instead of turning into that room, though, she kept going.

"Do you know what's down here?" Harper asked.

"No. Do you?"

Harper shook her head and slipped her hand in Jared's. "No, but I haven't seen anyone come down here since we've been here. Either it's storage or they're hiding something good."

Jared snickered. "You're such a busybody."

"I think you have me confused with Zander."

"Zander is the king of busybodies," Jared clarified. "You might be the queen, though. Together you two are an unstoppable gossip force. When you add in Mel and Zander's mother, I honestly think the world could cease to exist because it will get swallowed into a gossip black hole."

Harper barked out a coarse laugh. "That is ridiculous," she said. "I don't gossip."

"You and Zander spent twenty minutes this past week talking about how Eric and Molly hold their shoulders when they talk to one another and what that could possibly mean regarding a future romance," Jared pointed out. "Are you saying that's not gossip?"

"That is an observation."

"Ten minutes after that you talked about how some hairdresser at the salon was getting a boob job and she was going to look like Dolly Parton if she wasn't careful," Jared said.

"That was … okay, that was gossip," Harper conceded. "Fine. I like to gossip. Sue me."

"As long as you admit it," Jared said, kissing Harper's cheek. "You're very cute when you get feisty."

"I'll keep that in mind when you try to get me to take another bubble bath and conveniently lose the soap and have to feel around the tub until you find it," Harper said, causing Jared to laugh.

"What? You don't like that game?"

"You keep looking in odd places for the soap," Harper said. "If the soap ended up where you were looking for it we'd have to call *Ripley's Believe It or Not* because it would be hopping soap."

"Given all the things you can do, I've learned never to rule anything out," Jared said, slipping his arm around Harper's waist and tugging her to him as he feigned seriousness. "I'll show you something else that hops later if you're a good girl."

"You're such a pig."

Jared and Harper moved down the hallway, following the bending corridor until it led them into an ornate ballroom. Harper sucked in a breath when she saw it, the pink walls and exquisite chandeliers knocking her for a loop.

"Wow," Jared said, releasing Harper so he could move farther into the room. "I had no idea this was here. This is so … ."

"Beautiful," Harper enthused, her eyes wide as she tried to drink everything in.

"I was going to say tacky and ostentatious, but we can go with your word," Jared said, grinning when Harper shot him an evil look. "It's just so … pink."

"That's because it was designed in the 1970s," Harper said, moving to the nearby wall so she could study the photographs on display. "Wow. Look at this. That's William Milliken. He was Michigan's governor back in the eighties."

"How do you know that?" Jared asked, peering at the photograph. "He looks like your everyday random white dude."

Harper made a face. "My grandfather was obsessed with writing him letters," she said. "He used to complain about things he did all the time. I never understood why he was upset, but boy did he like mailing complaint letters."

Jared snickered. "I wish I could've met him. He sounds fun."

"I wish you could've met him, too," Harper said.

"Would he have liked me?"

"Since you're always making dirty suggestions, probably not," Harper said. "If you behaved yourself in his presence, he definitely would've liked you."

"Did he like Zander?"

"He loved Zander. He thought he was cheeky. That was the word he always used to describe him."

"Zander is definitely cheeky," Jared said. "I can think of a few other words to describe him, too."

"Don't be mean about my Zander," Harper chided, moving to the next photograph. "No way."

"What?" Jared followed Harper and widened his eyes when he saw the photograph. "Is that Sonny Bono?"

"That looks to be after his *Sonny & Cher* days but before his political days," Harper said. "I wonder if he had ties to Michigan."

"That would be my guess," Jared said. "Oh, look, the eighties came to the Stokes' house. Even the rich weren't spared the atrocity of eighties hairstyles."

Harper laughed as she stared at the three women in the photo. Their hair was as wide as it was long. She leaned forward after a moment, frowning as she tried to get a better look at the woman on the far right.

"What's wrong?" Jared asked.

"I can't be sure, but I'm almost positive this is the ghost I saw today," Harper said, pointing.

Jared knit his eyebrows together and stared at the woman in question. She was pretty, beautiful even. Her hair was long and tinged with red highlights. Even though her hairstyle was ridiculous by today's standards, you could tell she was the belle of whatever ball she was attending.

"Are you sure?"

"I'm sure," Harper said. "That's her. It's weird. I told Zander her clothes seemed dated and he was horrified to think she might be trapped in the eighties for all of eternity."

"Did the ghost look the same age as this woman?" Jared asked, pointing.

"Pretty close," Harper said. "I think the ghost looked like she was in her twenties or thirties. She might have been younger. I honestly didn't get a good look at her because I was so amped up due to the storm."

Jared removed the frame from the wall and turned it over. "I was hoping there would be some identifying card or something, but I guess not."

"Open it," Harper instructed. "My grandmother always writes the names of people on the back of the photographs, not the frames. Most people don't have boxes of photographs hanging around these days so it's kind of fallen out of habit, but if there's going to be any sort of identifying marker on there, it will be inside of the frame."

Jared did as Harper asked, pulling the cardboard buffer out and smiling when he saw cursive handwriting. "It looks like you were right ... again."

"You should just assume I'm always right and reward me accordingly," Harper said, glancing at the names. "Janet Marcil, Theresa Coolidge, and Alice Thorpe. According to this, my ghost's name is Alice."

Jared flipped the photograph over again and studied the three faces. "I didn't realize it right off, but Janet Marcil is Josh's mother," he said. "She looks a lot different now, but that's her."

Harper stared at the brunette in question. "When did she die?"

"She's not dead," Jared said. "Well, at least as far as I know. Josh didn't mention losing his mother so I assume she's still alive."

"I haven't seen her," Harper said. "Linden has been all over the place. He's been playing a part in the murder mysteries and hanging out with the guests. I guess I just assumed Josh's mother was gone because she hasn't put in an appearance."

"She's never been what I would call a fun person," Jared said, putting the frame back together so he could replace it on the wall. "I only met her a few times when we were in college and each time she came to visit it was as if someone made her come."

"That doesn't sound like most mothers I know," Harper said. "Why do you think she was so unpleasant?"

"I have no idea," Jared answered, straightening the frame so it matched in with the others. "Linden was always happy and wanted to hear about all of our college shenanigans. Janet wanted to be anywhere but near us."

"That's sad," Harper said. "My mother drives me nuts, but at least she's interested in my life. Of course, in the case of my mother, she might be a little too interested."

"I think she's funny," Jared said. "She reminds me of my mother in some ways, although I think it's harder for mothers and daughters to relate than sons and mothers. Mothers and daughters fight because they're so much alike while mothers dote on their sons."

"Are you saying I'm like my mother?"

Jared didn't like the tone of Harper's voice. He recognized a trap when he saw one. "I'm saying that you're my favorite person in the world."

"Nice save, but now I'm going to wonder if you're seeing my mother whenever we do … stuff. Thanks for giving me nightmares."

Jared involuntarily shuddered. "And thank you for putting that image in my head. That was mean."

"I think you deserved it," Harper said, grinning. "I … oh, hey, Josh. We were just looking around."

Jared swiveled when he realized they weren't alone anymore, offering Josh a sheepish smile. "I'm sorry if we're intruding, but we wanted to take a walk after dinner and our options were kind of limited," he said. "We ended up here. I hope it's not a problem."

"It's not a problem," Josh said, moving closer to Harper and Jared. "No one ever comes in this room. It's a shame."

"How come you're not using it for the mystery event?" Harper asked. "The guests would love it."

"Yes, well, I would love it, too," Josh said. "Unfortunately my mother would have kittens – not metaphorical kittens, real ones, mind you – if anyone dared have a good time in her beloved ballroom."

"We were just talking about your mother," Jared said, gesturing toward the photograph. "Harper assumed she was dead because we haven't seen her. Is she out of town?"

"Oh, no, she's here," Josh said, making a face. "She's ensconced in her suite because she can't be bothered to mingle with the little people."

"Tell us how you really feel," Jared teased. "Is everything okay?"

Josh blew out a frustrated sigh. "My mother is having the toughest time adjusting to our new reality," he said. "I love my mother, but … she's difficult. She's always been fairly distant with me and I have no idea how to talk to her.

"When this all went down she was living in denial," he continued. "She didn't want to see what was right in front of her and it was hard to explain something she had no interest in understanding."

"Did you think you could magically turn the money situation around without sacrifice?" Harper asked, her heart going out to Josh. He was obviously struggling with his mother's part in his life. She struggled with her mother, too, but it was nowhere near the degree Josh struggled.

"My mother never went to college and she has no head for business," Josh replied. "She always spent money and never gave a thought to where it was coming from or what would happen if it stopped pouring in. It was ... unfortunate ... when things took a slide.

"It didn't help that my father hid the realities of what was happening from her for a good six months," he continued. "She spent money we didn't have to lose during that entire time. She bought two cars and took expensive vacations. It was a nightmare.

"When I came home and found out what was going on I basically had to put her on an allowance," Josh said. "It was quite small, especially when compared to what she was getting before. I sold some of her stuff and took away her credit cards. She pretty much looks at me as the enemy now.

"That was just the beginning, though," he said. "When we decided to turn the house into a hotel she pitched a fit to rival the biggest divas in the world. She screamed and yelled and threw things. She demanded that we figure out something else to do – and give her the credit cards back – and when I told her this was our last shot she called me a liar and stormed out.

"She barely speaks to me now, and when I asked to use the ballroom for the mystery event, she pretty much threatened to stab me in the neck if I even tried," he continued. "I decided it wasn't worth the hassle and let go of the ballroom idea. Things are fine with the space we have, but it would've been nice to have a dance party in here on the final night."

"Holy crap," Jared said. "What does your father say about all this?"

"My father does his best, but he's unwilling to even discuss anything with my mother," Josh answered. "They're pretty much living separate lives. They even sleep in different bedrooms."

"That's sad," Jared said. "I'm sorry you're dealing with so much."

"I'm sorry, too," Harper said.

"It is what it is," Josh said. "I can't change it so I live with it. Out of curiosity, though, how come you were looking at my mother's photograph?"

"Oh, I was curious about this woman," Harper said, pointing to Alice. "She looks familiar for some reason, but I can't seem to place where I think I know her from."

Josh shrugged. "I have no idea who she is," he said finally. "I've never seen her before. I've never even really looked at the photos in this room. It's a little too pink for my liking, although I did skateboard in here one time and I legitimately thought my mother's head was going to pop off when she found out. I can't help you with that woman, though. I'm sorry."

Harper was disappointed but not surprised. At best Josh would've been an infant when Alice Thorpe died. "That's okay," she said. "I was just curious."

Jared wasn't ready to let it go. "We opened the frame because Harper is a curious little thing and it said the woman's name was Alice Thorpe. Does that ring any bells?"

Josh wrinkled his nose. "I don't think so," he said. "I can ask my father if it's important."

"It's not important," Harper said, shaking her head to send Jared a silent warning. "I was simply curious. She probably just has one of those familiar faces that make people think they recognize her when they really don't."

"Probably," Josh said. "I came to find you guys because they're about to discover another body. This one is the mistress of the man who died earlier. It's going to be very soap opera-y. You don't want to miss it."

"We definitely don't want to miss that," Jared said, reaching for Harper's hand. "We're still going to bed early, though. Don't forget that."

"I would expect nothing less."

FOURTEEN

Jared woke up to the sound of voices the next morning. He figured it was Zander and Harper doing their regular ritual and discarded it as he tried to drift back off, but a rumble of thunder jerked him back to reality.

"Wait a second."

Jared rolled to his side and found Harper sitting with her back propped up against the pillows. Her cell phone was on top of her bent knees and she was Skyping with Zander.

"You have got to be kidding me," Jared grumbled. "Even when we're on vacation he ends up in bed with us."

"We're talking about serious business things," Harper said. "I'm sorry, but he needed a few answers and I promised I would be available to help him if things popped up. You heard us say we were going to Skype every morning. I didn't think it would be a problem."

"No, I'm sorry," Jared offered, rubbing the sleep from his eyes. "I didn't realize it was business."

"Well, it is," Harper said. "Go on, Zander."

"So, anyway, I call Eric to tell him not to bother coming in to work today because of the weather and ... well ... we have no clients, which is a whole other issue, and I swear I heard a woman in the background," Zander said. "She called his name and said that breakfast was ready."

"Maybe it was his mother."

"Mothers don't giggle like that when they're with their sons," Zander replied. "It's unnatural ... and potentially gross and illegal."

"How is this about work?" Jared asked.

"Eric is my employee," Harper replied, unruffled. "That makes it about work."

"I don't ever want to hear you say that you don't gossip again," Jared chided shifting so he could prop himself up next to Harper and get a gander at Zander through the tiny screen. He wanted to laugh because Zander was in his pajamas and still in bed. In a way, it was like they all really were in bed together. "Harper claimed she doesn't gossip last night. How do you feel about that?"

Zander snorted. "If we didn't gossip, we'd have absolutely nothing to talk about except for your nipples and my good looks."

"I told you," Jared said, his eyes flashing as he ignored the dig about his nipples. "How are things in Whisper Cove? Is Mel holding up the fort without me?"

"Uncle Mel is fine," Zander answered. "He misses your handsome face, but when I told him about your abnormally large nipples he got uncomfortable and hung up. You've got that reaction to look forward to when you get back, Jared."

"I can't wait," Jared deadpanned, glancing at the window. "It's really coming down out there again. When I heard you guys talking I assumed it was another morning in Harper's bed because I was confused, and then I heard the storm and remembered where I was."

"We actually do have a legitimate reason to talk," Harper said.

"Yes, Harper misses me and can't live without me," Zander said. "You need to remember that."

"I'm well aware of that," Jared said. "Did you have another reason for calling?"

"I did," Harper confirmed. "I wanted Zander to see if he could convince Eric to run a search on Alice Thorpe."

"That's actually a good idea," Jared said, rubbing his hand over his stubbled jaw. "That's a really good idea. I thought you could ask

Linden if we ran into him today, but you shut me down on that pretty quickly last night. How come?"

"Josh is dealing with enough and if Linden is going through half as much as his son, he's already got a lot on his plate," Harper explained. "Besides that, if something terrible happened to Alice Thorpe, asking questions about her is going to rile some feathers if we're not careful."

"What do you mean?"

"Think about it," Harper prodded. "Alice Thorpe's ghost is here. When I asked her where she was going to be she pointed at the cemetery. If she has no ties to the Stokes family – and she must not if Josh doesn't know who she is – how did she end up dead out here?"

"That's actually a very good question," Jared said. "Maybe the answer is simple. Maybe Alice died in an accident. Maybe Josh doesn't know about her because no one ever talks about the accident. We don't know it's a murder."

"We don't," Harper agreed. "We don't know it's not a murder either."

"Most ghosts hang around because something really bad happened to them," Zander offered. "We've had a few accidents keep people around, and even fewer people die in their sleep and just get confused so they hang on. The vast majority of ghosts remain behind because they died violently and want revenge."

"Okay, let's talk about that," Jared said. "If Alice was murdered, we're thinking it was sometime in the eighties, right?"

"How old is Josh?" Harper asked.

"He was born in 1988."

"Okay, if Alice died here in the eighties and Josh was born in 1988, she could've conceivably died before Josh's birth," Harper said. "Her hair indicates eighties fashion, but when I saw her ghost it was still big but somehow tamed from what we saw in that photograph."

"The eighties really were unkind to fashion," Zander mused. "I wonder who thought of ratting hair and overdosing on Aqua Net, took a look in the mirror and said 'that looks awesome, we should start a trend' and then showed that hairstyle to other people? It's just unnatural."

Harper couldn't stop herself from giggling and even Jared was amused. "People toned down the ratting late in the eighties but still had big hair, right?" she asked.

"Pretty much," Zander replied. "I'm not an expert on the era because I think it should be wiped from the history books, but that sounds about right."

"That would mean she died in the late eighties," Jared supplied. "Once the nineties and Nirvana hit, the excess of the eighties was a thing of the past and angst and pouting of the slacker generation was the new trend."

"Ah, the introduction of flannel as a legitimate fashion choice instead of the last resort for lumberjacks," Zander said. "That was also a horrible time for fashion."

"I'm guessing Alice died after Josh's birth, but there's no way of knowing until we can talk to her," Harper said. "There's no way to find her until these storms pass. Do we know more about when they're going to end?"

"I think they're supposed to roll through all day," Zander answered. "I slept like a baby last night. I love a good thunderstorm. Was it loud out on the island?"

"I couldn't hear over Harper's snoring," Jared replied.

"I do not snore," Harper said, playfully slapping Jared's arm. "That's you."

"I didn't snore," Jared argued. "After our bath, I was out like a light."

"Yes, Harper told me about your baths and the hopping soap," Zander said. "That's very original."

Jared shot Harper a disgusted look. "Do you have to tell him everything?"

"Pretty much."

"Can't you leave a few things for just you and me to know about?" Jared prodded. "I'm not talking about everything, just a few things."

"I guess," Harper said, giving in. "Do you want to take a shower and not tell him about it?"

"You just told him about it," Jared pointed out.

"That was an accident."

"Whatever," Jared made a face and turned his attention back to

Zander. "If you find anything out about Alice Thorpe, give us a call. I'm not sure where to look for information on her and we don't exactly have access to computers out here."

"I'm on it," Zander said. "I'm bored anyway. It will probably be the most fun I have all day, which is a little sad. Maybe I'll turn a *Real Housewives of Beverly Hills* marathon on to entertain myself while I'm doing it."

"Don't be a cliché," Harper said.

"It's not being cliché when I make fun of them," Zander said. "I can't seem to help myself."

"Okay, well ... make sure and mock them for me, too," Harper said.

"I definitely will."

"Other than that, I think we're all caught up," Jared said, reaching for the phone.

"What are you doing?" Zander asked, wrinkling his nose. "Don't you even think about disconnecting that phone. I'm not done talking to Harper yet."

"Oh, you're done talking to Harper," Jared said. "It's time for us to do something private and for you to be cut out of the information highway. We'll call you if we get anything ... and I'm pretty sure Harper will call you this afternoon when she thinks I'm not looking because she'll want to gossip again."

"Don't you hang up that phone," Zander warned.

"Goodbye, Zander."

"You still have huge nipples!"

JOSH WAS ALREADY SEATED AT WHAT HARPER HAD COME TO consider "their" table when she and Jared made their way into the dining room shortly before nine. He greeted them with a wide smile and pushed the carafe of coffee in their direction.

"You two look happy this morning," he said. "Did you have fun going to bed early last night?"

"I'm not answering that question on the grounds that it might upset Harper and I don't want to risk that in case I need a nap this afternoon," Jared answered, pouring mugs of coffee for both of them. "How was the murder mystery event after we left?"

"Oh, well, the guests had fun going through the clues regarding the affair," Josh answered. "They were pretty spicy. I have to hand it to the guy who wrote them because there was a lot of giggling and suggestive winks."

"Oh, really?" Harper asked, sipping her coffee. "How did that go over?"

"Let's just say you and Jared weren't the only ones to retire early and leave it at that, shall we?"

"I'm fine with that," Jared said. "What's the news on the weather? Zander filled us in a little bit, but he's prone to dramatic fits so I want to hear it from you just to be on the safe side."

"You already talked to Zander this morning?" Josh asked, his eyes lighting up. "Did you talk to each other as a group, or was this an individual thing?"

"I know what you're thinking and I don't care if you make fun of me," Jared said. "I woke up to Harper and Zander talking and thought I was back at Harper's house. It turns out they were Skyping – ostensibly about work – and they had gossip to share. We also talked about the weather."

"How fun," Josh said, smirking. "Well, as for the weather, we're definitely stuck here for the day. The storms are supposed to roll through with breaks in between, but even during the breaks it's supposed to drizzle.

"The ferry is not making any crossings today and there's a good chance it won't tomorrow either," he continued. "It's probably a good thing that this event is scheduled to go on for a few more days, because if people wanted to leave and couldn't we would be in a world of hurt."

"That's true," Harper said, leaning back in her chair. "Does this affect that game at all? Were any of the clues outside?"

"We were going to have a body discovered in the stable, but that's definitely out," Josh answered. "Instead we're moving things to the third floor and doing it up there. That allows everyone to spread out looking for clues."

"That's probably a good thing," Jared said. "I have a feeling that this group is going to make me feel claustrophobic after being trapped for a few hours under the same roof together. They're nice people, but they're odd."

"You just told me that you Skyped from bed with your girlfriend and her best friend and you all gossiped together," Josh pointed out. "Who is weird in that scenario?"

Jared frowned. "You're right," he said. "You've turned me into a weirdo, Heart. I hope you're happy."

"No one made you gossip with us," Harper pointed out. "You're the one who told him we were showering together. Now he's going to want details when he calls this afternoon and you're going to have to be there to supply them because I'm not allowed to tell him on my own thanks to your new decree about keeping some things in our relationship private."

"You're talking to him again this afternoon?" Josh was flabbergasted. "When did you turn into a girl, man?"

"Don't demean him," Harper chided. "You shouldn't use the word 'girl' as a derogatory term, by the way. I'm a girl and I happen to like being a girl."

"I happen to like that you're a girl, too," Jared said, his smile charming. "This would be a very different relationship if you weren't."

"You can say that again," Josh said, shaking his head. "I can't believe you. You're so … smitten. It's sick."

"I am smitten," Jared agreed, fondly tugging on a strand of Harper's hair. "I didn't expect it, but it really is great."

"I guess I'm really happy for you then," Josh said. "I should probably stop hitting on your girlfriend, huh? If you're smitten, it would be mean to go after her."

"I don't care if you go after her," Jared said. "You'll never catch her, though. She's too good for you."

"But she's not too good for you?"

"She's probably too good for me, too," Jared conceded. "That doesn't mean I'm letting her go, though. I haven't been with her long, but I already know I would be lost without her."

"Ugh," Harper intoned, making a face. "That's the sweetest thing I've ever heard."

"I know. I think I'm going to be sick," Josh deadpanned. "You two have given me indigestion."

"Well, I'm starving," Harper said, her eyes locked on Jared's. "I already know how I'm going to work off this big meal, though, and it has absolutely nothing to do with walking."

"And that's why I adore you," Jared said, shifting his head so he could scan the dining room. "Where is the waiter? We've got a schedule to keep."

"Yup, I'm definitely going to be sick," Josh said.

FIFTEEN

"They look happy."

Linden moved up next to Josh and smiled as he watched Harper and Jared snuggle in a corner chair in the lobby later that morning. They had a book open, but there wasn't a lot of reading going on. Instead there was a lot of kissing and giggling going on, and whatever they kept whispering to one another was amusing both of them enough that they managed to tune out the rest of the guests and forge their own little world.

"They do look happy," Josh agreed, his expression rueful. "I never thought Jared would be the settling down type. I thought he would find it boring. He always had a restless spirit. He doesn't look bored, though, does he?"

Linden chuckled. "He certainly doesn't look bored."

The two men lapsed into comfortable silence for a moment, smiling in unison when Harper chortled thanks to a shared joke.

"Do you want to tell me what's wrong?" Linden asked, turning his full attention to his son. "You seem … sad."

"Nothing is wrong," Josh said hurriedly. "I'm glad everyone is here … and I'm especially glad Jared is here."

"You're feeling wistful," Linden prodded. "You thought you had antsy feet until you saw Jared's feet planted firmly on the ground. You thought he was playing a joke when he told you he was bringing a girlfriend. Even when you first met her you thought it was an extended game.

"You've watched them for a few days now and you realize it's not a game," he continued. "You were happy with your life because you thought it was what you wanted until you saw Jared living another life and now you're wondering if you would be happier living another life."

"That was quite the mouthful," Josh joked.

"Am I wrong?"

Josh sighed as Jared tickled Harper's ribs and she bit her lip to muffle a squeal. They really did look euphoric. "You're not wrong," he said. "I didn't realize that I might want a relationship until it became apparent that I was missing out by not having one.

"I've never seen Jared this happy," he continued. "He was a real ladies' man in college. The women swooned when he was around. He was always pleasant and respectful around them, but you could tell settling down wasn't on his mind.

"He never had a girlfriend," Josh said. "He was never in a real relationship. I think Harper is the only one he's ever really bonded with enough to form a relationship."

"Does that bother you?"

"Why would it bother me?" Josh asked evasively.

"I've seen you with Jared and Harper," Linden said. "You keep making jokes about going after her, but I think part of you would if she wasn't with one of your oldest friends."

"Harper is great," Josh said. "She's with Jared, though. I'm only flirting with her to drive him crazy. That's the way things go between us. It's a guy thing."

"I'm well aware of how the male brain works," Linden said, chuckling. "While I'm not advocating going after Harper – and I'm really not because she's clearly taken – you could always find someone else to form a relationship with."

"There's a lot going on around here right now," Josh said. "That's a concern for another time."

"You can't run away from love, son," Linden said. "It will find you no matter what. I get the distinct impression Jared wasn't looking for love when he found Harper, and yet look at them now."

"And look at you and Mom," Josh challenged. "Relationships are great when you're floating on clouds like Jared and Harper. What happens when things shift and the love disappears? I don't have time for distractions right now. That might change down the road, but for now I have to focus on the business."

"I understand that," Linden said. "Don't sell your personal life short to propel your business life, though. I learned the hard way about that. You won't find happiness down that road. You need to find a way to balance both desires."

"I'll take that under consideration," Josh said. "Until then I'm going to see to our guests. If this storm doesn't ease up soon everyone is going to start committing real murders out of boredom."

"Well, at least it would be a change of pace," Linden quipped.

"THIS BEING 'RAINED IN' TOGETHER ISN'T SUCH A BAD THING," Jared said, pressing his palm against Harper's flat abdomen as he snuggled her close and nuzzled her neck. "It's giving me ideas."

"You don't need a storm to give you those ideas," Harper teased. "You have those ideas twenty-four hours a day."

"I guess I can't argue with that," Jared said, brushing Harper's hair out of her face. "I still have ideas."

"Before we get to your ideas, I need to run to the bathroom," Harper said, playfully nipping the corner of Jared's mouth. "If you wait for me to finish that task I promise to play whatever game you're cooking up in that perverted mind of yours."

"Whatever game?" Jared challenged, arching an eyebrow. "That could be a dangerous assertion, little lady."

"Whatever game," Harper confirmed. "I really have to go to the bathroom, though. I don't know if it's the sound of the rain coming down outside or what, but my bladder is starting to complain loud enough to drown everything else out."

"Then go," Jared said, playfully swatting Harper's rear end and pushing her to a standing position. "I'll be here thinking of a game to play. Keep in mind that the longer you take in the bathroom, the more time I'll have to let my diabolical nature come out to play. You've been warned."

"You have the oddest sense of humor sometimes," Harper said, dropping a quick kiss on Jared's mouth before heading toward the restroom.

Jared wasn't alone long because Josh settled in the nearby chair moments after Harper vacated the area.

"Were you waiting for Harper to leave so you could talk to me privately?" Jared asked, already knowing the answer.

"Of course not," Josh said, shaking his head. "You looked lonely without your blonde. I was just filling in until she returns."

"That's not what you're doing and we both know it," Jared said. "You want to know what happened by the road and you're trying to decide if you should bring it up or let it go. You forget that I know you. You're a curious guy. You can't let things like this go, and I get it. It really is nothing, though."

"Jared, I know you've pretty much fallen head over heels for her, but she was talking to air," Josh said, keeping his voice low. "She was having a conversation with someone only she could see. Are you honestly saying that doesn't worry you?"

Jared licked his lips as he bought himself time to decide how to answer. "Are you worried that she's crazy for talking to herself or I'm crazy for being with her?"

Josh's eyebrows shot up his forehead. "I wasn't insinuating either," he protested. "I like Harper. She seems fun and she makes you laugh. That's good enough for me no matter what. I would be lying if I said that her staring at a bare spot in the driveway and talking to someone who obviously wasn't there as a storm was about to hit wasn't trouble-some, but that's your business."

"And yet you're over here making it your business," Jared challenged. "Listen, man, I know you've only got my best interests at heart, but you really are out of line. Harper is a good person – and I promise she's completely sane. Er, well, mostly sane. There are times when she gets together with Zander where I'm certain they should be locked up in a mental ward. Other than that, though, she is not only sane but bright and intelligent."

"I'm happy you've found her," Josh said. "I really am. She makes you smile and you seem almost ... delighted ... every time she opens her mouth. What I saw out at the road yesterday was really weird, though."

"I'm sure it was ... to you," Jared said. "I'm not bothered by it."

Josh's expression was thoughtful as he looked Jared up and down. "That's because you know what she was really doing, don't you?"

Jared feigned ignorance. "I have no idea what you mean."

"You know what she was doing out by the road," Josh said. "When you came in from your trip Harper made a beeline for you. You could tell she was upset and when I approached and told you what was going on you were surprised.

"At first I thought you were surprised to hear Harper was talking to herself and you went out of your way to cover for her," he continued. "That's not the case, though. You weren't surprised I told you what was going on. You were surprised by what was actually going on."

"I have no idea what you just said," Jared said truthfully. "You lost me somewhere in there."

"Harper has a secret," Josh said, knitting his eyebrows together. "Harper has a secret and you know it. Huh."

"Harper is an open book," Jared argued. "She doesn't have a secret."

"Oh, no, now I'm intrigued," Josh said. "Harper has a secret. I'm just dying to find out what it is."

HARPER WAS IN A GOOD MOOD WHEN SHE LEFT THE RESTROOM and turned back toward the lobby. Despite the weather and ghost – and the small part of her heart missing Zander, which she would never admit to Jared – she was having a great time.

She'd never been on vacation with a boyfriend before. It seemed weird to say given her age, but it was true. Before Jared showed up in her life, Harper made everything about GHI and Zander. Her parents wandered in and out when they were feeling dramatic or wanted attention, but it was a fairly boring life.

Jared changed all of that.

Harper was lost in her own mind – a few dirty games to play later with Jared flitting through her head – when she passed by the library. She thought it was empty until a flash of movement in the corner of the room caught her attention.

Harper turned back and walked into the library, internally sighing at the sheer beauty of the room as she focused on Hal Baker. She hadn't seen the man since his fake death to start the game, and he looked downtrodden as he peered out the window.

The lighting in the library wasn't great, most of the illumination coming from twin antique chandeliers, but Harper didn't miss the despondent look on Hal's face as she approached.

"You look like you've had better days," Harper said. "What's wrong? Does death have you down?"

"You have no idea." Hal didn't even bother glancing in Harper's direction.

"I hear your character was quite the cad," Harper said, watching Hal closely for clues to his mood. He seemed almost angry. She couldn't help but wonder if the weather was delaying his departure from the hotel. Since his character was already dead, he might not want to hang around for the rest of the game if he didn't have to. "Are you stuck here?"

"That would be my guess."

"The weather is supposed to break tomorrow," Harper offered. "I think they've pushed it off until later in the afternoon, but this will get better. Of course, the problem after that is the ferry. They won't resume operations until they're convinced the trip won't be choppy."

"I'm pretty sure I don't have to worry about that," Hal said, his gazed fixed on a point outside the window.

"Hal, is something wrong?" Harper asked, growing tired of his attitude and chilly conversational tactics. "If you need help with something ... or to talk ... ."

"That's pretty funny considering ... everything," Hal said, finally turning and locking gazes with Harper. "What should we talk about? I know. Let's talk about me being dead."

Harper was even more confused now than she was when they started the conversation. "Were you supposed to die later in the game or something? Is that why you're upset? If so, maybe I'm misunderstanding something, but it's still just a game. There's no reason to get your nose out of joint."

"Right. There's no reason to get my nose out of joint," Hal said, rolling his eyes with enough force Harper was surprised they didn't make a break for it and run away from his head. "There's no reason to be upset. I'm only dead. I should suck it up. Is that what you're saying?"

"I ... ." Harper tried to wrap her head around Hal's anger and look at things from his perspective. She often found that helpful when dealing with a situation she didn't fully understand. The problem was, when she did that, she still thought Hal was being ridiculous. "Maybe you should talk to one of the other actors," she suggested. "They might know how to make you feel better."

"Unless they're somehow magical and can bring me back from the dead, I don't see that happening," Hal said. "Now, do you mind? I was pouting alone and that's what I want to return to doing."

"Listen, Hal, you're obviously upset," Harper prodded. "There's no reason to take it out on me, though. I didn't decide the order of everyone's death. It's not like you're really dead. Get a little perspective."

"Perspective?" Hal's eyebrows nearly shot off his forehead. "Perspective?" He lifted his hand in front of the window and thanks to the added light – even though it was still muted – Harper realized what she'd missed upon first inspection.

"Oh, no."

"Yes, oh no," Hal deadpanned, wiggling is ethereal fingers in Harper's face for emphasis. "I'm not just fake dead. I'm really dead, too. Boo!"

SIXTEEN

"I have no idea what you're talking about," Jared said, striding down the hallway a few minutes later as he tried to put distance between himself and Josh. "Harper doesn't have a secret. She's the most honest person I know."

"You can say that with a straight face because you know the secret," Josh persisted. "I promise I won't tell anyone. You have to tell me what's going on. I think I've earned it."

"You're making stuff up in your head," Jared said. "There is no secret."

"I don't believe you."

"That's certainly your prerogative, but the fact remains that Harper is an open book," Jared said. "She doesn't have a secret. You're desperate to drum something up about her, though, so you're making up a secret to placate yourself."

"Then why are you running from me?" Josh asked, increasing his pace in case Jared tried to make a break for it. "If Harper doesn't have a secret, why did you all of a sudden develop a dire need to find Harper once I asked the question?"

"If you haven't noticed, Harper and I like to spend time together,"

Jared replied, choosing his words carefully. "If I'm out of her presence for more than a few minutes I start missing her."

"That makes you something of a wuss."

Jared scowled. "I know what you're trying to do and it's not going to work," he hissed. "There is no secret. Stop thinking there's a secret. You're imagining a secret when there's absolutely nothing there."

Jared took an involuntary step backward when Harper popped out of the library and grabbed his arm.

"I have to talk to you," Harper whispered, glancing at Josh. "It's kind of private. I'm sure you understand. It's a secret."

Josh crossed his arms over his chest and arched an eyebrow. "A secret, huh?"

"Ugh." Jared made an exasperated sound in the back of his throat. "You have the worst timing ever, Heart."

"I'm sorry," Harper said, tightening her grip on Jared's arm and tugging him into the library. "I have to talk to you, though."

"I'll leave you guys to it," Josh said. "Just keep in mind that if you do something filthy in that library and Trask finds out, he will plant you in the cemetery and try to cover up the crime."

"Wait," Harper said, shaking her head to still Josh before he could depart. "I need to talk to Jared, but then I have a feeling I'm going to need to talk to you. So, it would be really helpful if you would wait in the hallway and not eavesdrop."

"I'm sorry, what?" Josh was confused.

"I need you to wait here for a few minutes because we might need your help, but I have to talk to Jared alone first," Harper explained.

"Because you have a secret?" Josh said.

"I ... um ... sure," Harper said, giving in. She had no idea what point Josh was trying to prove, but she didn't have time to mess around. "Just give us a few minutes ... five tops."

"You want me to wait outside a closed library door, refrain from eavesdropping, and then do you a favor when you're done shutting me out?" Josh asked.

"Yes."

"How could I possibly turn down that offer?"

"You can't," Harper said, tugging on Jared's arm. "Come on. I ...

definitely have a problem." Harper closed the library door, shutting Josh out of their conversation while ushering Jared into a convoluted situation.

"What's wrong?" Jared asked. He didn't look particularly perturbed.

"First off, why was Josh following you?" Harper asked, ignoring Jared's question.

"He thinks you have a secret and I know what it is," Jared replied, not missing a beat. "I told him he was crazy and that you didn't have a secret. Then you announced you did have a secret and pulled me into the library. You're not doing a very good job of hiding things, Heart."

Harper sighed. "Well, crap. That doesn't really surprise me."

"What's second off?" Jared asked.

"What do you mean?"

"You said 'first off,' a few seconds ago," Jared said. "What's second off?"

"Oh, that," Harper muttered. "We have a problem."

"I can't wait to hear this," Jared said.

"I found another ghost."

"Okay," Jared said, unruffled. "Is it an old one like Alice, or a new one?"

"Oh, it's a new one," Harper said. "It's a very new one. In fact, I have a feeling it's so new we haven't discovered the body yet."

Jared realized what she was saying. "I'm not going to like this, am I?"

"Probably not."

"Just tell me," Jared said, resigned.

JARED'S FACE WAS UNREADABLE WHEN HE OPENED THE LIBRARY door again five minutes later. Josh trudged into the room, his gaze bouncing between Harper and Jared as he tried to get a handle on the situation.

"Do you want to let me in on the big secret?" Josh asked.

"We need you to tell us about the acting troupe," Jared said. "We … um … need to talk to Hal Baker."

"The guy running the troupe?" Josh asked, confused. "That's who you're talking about, right? He was the first guy to die."

"He was," Jared confirmed. "We talked to him after his body was discovered that first night. He seems like a good guy. Harper wants to hire him for one of her cemetery tours and we need to talk to him."

Josh was doubtful. "Are you going to look me in the eye and tell me Harper pulled you in that room because she wants to talk to Hal and you need my help finding him?"

"She also wanted to grope me when you weren't looking," Jared replied, smoothly sidestepping Harper's slap and smirking when she growled out her distaste for the conversational shift. "She's got busy hands. I personally don't mind them, but she's desperate for people to think she's a good girl. That's her deep, dark, and terrible secret."

"You know I don't believe that, right?" Josh asked.

"I know you're suspicious by nature and it's unnecessary," Jared answered. "I'm going to split the difference with you, though, because we really do need some help. I need to talk to Hal. It's very important. Did he have a room?"

"He stayed in the old servants' quarters," Josh answered. "The house has a basement level that has been renovated with staff rooms. Some of our staff stays here during seasonal months because it's mostly made up of teenagers. They stay in those rooms.

"When we decided to have the mystery troupe come for a visit, my dad figured we could rent out more rooms if the actors stayed in the basement," he continued. "The rooms are okay but not great. Hal and the other actors weren't thrilled with their accommodations, but it is what it is."

"We need to go down there," Jared said.

"Tell me why," Josh prodded.

"I ... ." Jared broke off, frustration evident as he glanced at Harper. "We have reason to believe something may have happened to Hal. I need to find him to make sure that's not the case."

Josh was surprised. "What could've happened to him?"

"We're not sure."

"Do you think he got lost in the storm or something?" Josh asked, refusing to acquiesce to Jared's demands without good reason. "Do you think he's ill?"

"I can't answer that right this second," Jared responded. "We need to see Hal's room. After that, well, we'll see what happens. Right now, though, it really is important that we see his room."

"And what if I demand an answer now?" Josh pressed.

"Then we'll find it on our own," Jared shot back. "I'm not playing a game here. We need to find Hal."

"Fine," Josh said, giving in. "You guys owe me an explanation for this later, though. I'm not joking."

"We'll take it under advisement," Jared said, holding out his hand to Harper. "Come on. We'll figure this out."

Josh was dying to know what "out" they were trying to figure, but he let it go for now. He couldn't push them too far before Jared started pushing back, and he wasn't sure if he was up to dealing with that.

"THIS room isn't so bad," Jared said, glancing around the basement abode. "I mean the view isn't great, but I don't see that there's anything to complain about when you've been hired to do a job."

"That's easy for him to say," Hal said, making a face as Jared poked through his things. "I heard you guys got one of the best rooms in the joint. Of course he's happy. He gets you and a great view. Who wouldn't be happy with that?"

Harper forced her face to remain neutral as she scanned Hal's space. The room was empty. She didn't expect to find him slumped on the ground or dead in his bed, but she was hopeful some sort of clue remained. Unfortunately, she couldn't ask Hal where to look because Josh insisted on visiting the room with them.

"We need to talk to some of the other people from the troupe," Harper said, keeping her voice low and neutral. "We have to find out when they spoke to him last."

"That's a good idea." Jared poked his head through the open doorway and glanced down both directions of the narrow hallway before he called out to someone. "Hey, can you come over here, please?"

Harper tilted her head to the side as she waited for a young woman to step into the room. She was pretty – almost ridiculously so – and she didn't appear bothered by Jared's request.

"Did you need something?" the woman asked.

"My name is Jared Monroe. I'm a police officer. What's your name?"

"Cara Sanders."

"Cara, you're a member of the mystery troupe, right?" Jared asked.

Cara nodded, flashing Jared a flirty smile as Harper rolled her eyes and bit her tongue to keep herself from saying something mean. "I'm going to win an Oscar one day," she said. "I'm going to be rich and famous. The mystery troupe is just my first stop."

"Congratulations," Jared said, completely uninterested in her future plans. "We need some information about Hal."

"What about him?" Cara asked, making a face. "He's been a pain in the ass since we got here. He thinks we're being mistreated because our rooms are in the basement, but these are a lot nicer rooms than we've had in other places we've stayed so I don't know what his deal is."

"She's always been a stuck up pain in the keister," Hal groused. "She thinks she's going to be an actress, but she can barely convince herself she's smart enough to cross the road without parental supervision, so I don't know how she thinks she's going to be an actress when you need powerful persuasion skills to pull off that job."

Harper snickered, catching herself before she let loose with a full laugh and pasted a serious look on her face when Josh's gaze landed on her.

"When was the last time you saw Hal?" Jared asked.

"Well, let me think," Cara said, winding a hank of hair around her finger as she leaned in closer to Jared and gave him a clear view down her top. Harper wanted to rip her hair out of her head and choke her with it. "It was yesterday," she said finally. "He was downstairs for dinner. I saw him in the dining room and then I didn't see him after that."

"Aren't the troupe actors supposed to stay out of sight after their make-believe deaths?" Harper asked. "Doesn't it ruin the mystique if they're sighted by the mystery solvers?"

"You would think that, but not really," Cara said, never moving her eyes from Jared's handsome face. "The people who come to these things take the games very seriously, but they also can manage to separate real life from fiction. Most of them don't care if we have dinner in the same area they do as long as we don't jerk them out of the game."

"Did Hal say anything to you yesterday about where he might be going after dinner?" Jared asked.

"Not that I recall," Cara replied.

"And you haven't seen him since, right?" Josh asked.

Cara shook her head. "I didn't even realize I hadn't seen him until you mentioned it," she said. "It's kind of strange. He usually checks in with us several times a day."

"Well, thank you," Jared said. "If you think of anything else, we'll be around."

"Is Hal in some kind of trouble?" Cara asked.

"Like she cares," Hal muttered, crossing his ghostly arms over his chest.

"He's not in trouble," Jared replied. "We're just trying to find him. It's important."

"Well, I hope you find him them," Cara said, moving toward the door. "By the way, if you're looking for someone to share dinner with tonight, I'm available."

Josh chuckled while Harper made a disgusted face.

"Thank you for the offer," Jared said. "I have dinner plans with my favorite blonde, though."

Cara wrinkled her nose and glanced at Harper. "Do you mean her?"

"I do."

"Did I mention I'm going to be a famous actress one day?" Cara pressed. "You should really get in with me now because you'll be kicking yourself if you don't when I'm rich and famous."

"That's … an interesting offer," Jared said. "I happen to adore my blonde, though. I think I'm going to stick with her."

"It's your loss," Cara said, Jared's esteem diminishing in her eyes.

She turned her attention to Josh. "You own this place, right? That must mean you're rich. Do you want to have dinner later?"

Josh kept his face even despite the surreal nature of the question. "I think I'm going to stick with the blonde, too."

"Suit yourself," Cara said, annoyed as she strode toward the door. "I guess there's no accounting for taste."

"She should know," Hal muttered.

"I know, right?" Harper said. She realized too late that she'd responded to Hal's dig in front of Josh.

"You know what?" Josh asked.

Harper's face drained of color as she struggled for something — anything really – that would fix the situation. "I … ."

"Heart, it's okay," Jared said quietly.

"What is going on?" Josh asked. He was on the verge of exploding. "Someone had better tell me what the big deal is right now or I'm going to assume Harper is a cyborg with a radio planted in her head."

"I'm not a cyborg," Harper said.

"Thanks," Josh said dryly. "I never would've figured that one out on my own."

"I can, however, see and talk to ghosts," Harper said, rolling her neck until it cracked as she braced herself for Josh's imminent melt-down. "Hal is dead. He's standing right next to me. He can't remember where his body is. We need to find it and then make sure the other guests are safe because you have a murderer on the loose."

Josh's mouth dropped open as he took Harper's admission in.

"Wow, I feel so much better," Harper said.

"I don't think that guy does," Hal said, waving an invisible hand in Josh's face. "In fact, if I didn't know better, I would think he's about to pass out."

SEVENTEEN

It was as if all the oxygen had been sucked out of the room.

"Can you repeat that?" Josh said, finally finding his voice after what felt like eons of uncomfortable silence. "I think I may have misheard you ... or had a stroke."

"I'm pretty sure you didn't mishear me," Harper countered. "If you need time to wrap your head around all of this, though, I understand. For the record – and for those with wax buildup in their ears – I can see and talk to ghosts."

"But ... ." Josh broke off and glanced at Jared. "Did you talk her into doing this so I would learn my lesson about prying?"

"No." Jared's face was unreadable as he kept his eyes on Josh and reached out for Harper's hand. "Come here, Heart."

Harper took Jared's proffered support and moved closer to him. She understood what he was doing – building a protective wall around her with his mere presence – but she was hopeful it wouldn't be necessary.

"This has to be a joke," Josh said, shaking his head. "You're messing with me."

"I'm not messing with you," Jared said. "Harper can see and talk to ghosts. It's true."

"And you believe this?" Josh looked as if he was thirty seconds away from calling the men with the straightjackets to haul Harper and Jared off to a padded room. "You believe she can talk to ghosts? Forgive me if I find that a little hard to believe."

"I understand this is probably difficult for you," Harper said. "Jared wanted to tell you the truth from the beginning, but I was the reticent one. I wanted one weekend of peace and quiet without people looking at me like I'm crazy ... just like you're doing now."

"I'm sorry if you think that's how I'm looking at you, but ... well, I might be looking at you a little bit that way," Josh conceded. "It's just ... that is the most ludicrous thing I've ever heard. Jared, you're a police officer. How can you believe that pile of crap?"

"Because it's the truth," Jared replied evenly.

"Are you pretending to believe it because she gives you sex?" Josh pressed. "I mean, I guess that makes sense in the grand scheme of things. She is hot."

Jared scowled. "I'm not pretending to believe it. I honestly do believe it. Harper is gifted."

"But ... that's just ... you can't possibly ... this is unbelievable." Josh couldn't grasp a coherent thought to anchor himself with.

"Josh, Harper was nervous about admitting what she could do because you and I have been friends for a long time," Jared explained. "She's usually pretty forthcoming with stuff like this. She owns a ghost hunting business, after all, and she doesn't generally hide who she is.

"She was uncomfortable telling you even though I told her you would understand and accept her gifts from the start," he continued. "I'm starting to rethink that belief given your current attitude, but she was worried and wanted a problem-free week."

"And what changed?" Josh asked. "Did Casper climb in the bathtub with you guys?"

"No," Jared said, making a face.

"That might explain your hopping soap theory, though," Harper mused.

Jared didn't want to smile and yet he couldn't help himself. "See. I told you it was a legitimate phenomenon."

"Wait, so you guys just expect me to swallow this ghost thing whole and not question you on it?" Josh asked. "If so, I've got a rude awakening for you, because this is the dumbest thing I've ever heard in my entire life."

"And I've got a rude awakening for you," Harper said, refusing to back down. "Hal Baker is dead. He remembers going to dinner yesterday, but he can't remember anything after that. He woke up in the library, but I looked around and couldn't find a body or any sign of a struggle. His body is out there somewhere and we need to find it."

"Did you hire Hal to do this?" Josh asked. "I would deserve it if you did. I've been something of a pain to you guys because I thought Harper was hiding something. This is a great way to pay me back. Ha, ha. You got me."

Harper rubbed her forehead as she tried to figure out a way to make Josh see the truth without completely losing his mind in the process. Jared stepped in and took the decision away from her.

"We're not joking with you," Jared said. "If we were, we would've owned up to it by now. As it happens, you're making Harper more and more uncomfortable with each ill-conceived word you spout. I don't need you making her feel bad about this. She's amazing, and you're the one looking like a douche for having a problem."

"Jared, it's okay," Harper said, keeping her voice low. "I'm honestly used to this. That's why I knew he wouldn't be as cool about everything as you thought he would be."

"But … ." Josh's face was plaintive as his eyes bounced between Harper and Jared. "Seriously, this is the best prank ever. When did you guys think of this? Is this what you were talking about in the library when Harper grabbed you?"

Jared shook his head, disgusted, and then turned his full attention to Harper. "We need a map of the property and blueprints for the house," he said. "I want Hal to have something to look at to jar his memory. For all we know he died of natural causes – yes, I remember what Zander said and know that's not the norm, but it's still a possibility – but we need Hal to remember where his body is."

"You cannot be serious," Josh muttered, flabbergasted.

"There's a map of the grounds in the library," Harper said. "I saw it when I was in there earlier."

"We'll start there then," Jared said, grabbing Harper's hand and moving toward the door. "When you get over yourself, Josh, you'll be able to find us in the library. Don't bother following us unless you're ready to apologize to Harper. I'm not kidding."

"DO YOU SEE ANYTHING ON THIS MAP YOU RECOGNIZE?" Harper asked Hal ten minutes later, fighting to keep her voice pleasant even though she wanted to strangle the temperamental ghost.

"If I knew where I died I would tell you," Hal said. "I'm not playing games. Trust me. The last thing I want to do is leave my body out there to rot so I won't be able to have an open casket."

"Ugh," Harper said, making a face. "Why would you want an open casket?"

"Why not?" Hal asked.

"Because people will be looking at you when you're dead and it's weird," Harper answered. "Study that map and make sure nothing looks familiar. We're at a dead end if you can't remember where you died."

Harper ambled over to the chair Jared sat in and rested her hand on his wrist. He flashed her a warm smile when he glanced up, but Harper could read the worry in the depths of his eyes.

"I'm sorry for what I did," Harper said. "I knew it was a mistake, but I was tired and I didn't want to play games when I knew there was a body out there to be found. I should've found a better way. What I did was ... absolutely moronic."

"You didn't do anything stupid," Jared argued, patting his lap to entice Harper to sit down. Harper did just that and Jared wrapped his arms around her waist and cuddled her close as they waited for Hal to come up with a solution to his missing body problem. "I honestly thought he would understand."

"Jared, I've been through this a few times in my life, and he's not acting differently than most other people," Harper said. "No one ever believes I can do what I do right off the bat. That takes time."

"What about your parents?"

"They didn't believe me and my mother thought I was troubled when I told her my grandfather visited me the night he died," Harper replied. "My father would play along when I was little – like the ghosts were my imaginary friends – but I know he didn't really believe me at the time. It meant a lot that he pretended to, though. I think that's why I get along with him better than my mom. She took longer to believe me ... and she was harsh about her disbelief when she wanted to be."

"They eventually came to believe, though."

"They did," Harper confirmed. "After knowing things I shouldn't have been able to know so many times they lost count, they ultimately gave in and embraced it. I wouldn't exactly call either of them proud, but they stand up for me now and they believe."

Jared traced Harper's high cheekbone with his thumb as he studied her profile. "What about Zander?"

"He believed from the beginning," Harper said, smiling at the memory. "He never once doubted what I could do. He claims he fell in love with me the moment he saw me and knew we were going to be best friends forever. It took me longer to fall in love with him because I always worried about what people thought about me, even before I could see ghosts."

"You don't seem to have that problem now," Jared said. "Well, for the most part, I mean. I thought you were being ridiculous when you insisted on telling everyone you ran haunted ghost tours for a living. I didn't ... understand ... what you went through.

"I do now," he continued. "I'm sorry. I should've listened to you. I won't make that mistake again."

"I learned about self-esteem as I grew older," Harper said. "It wasn't a lesson I sought out. It just kind of ... happened. I think Zander was a big part of it because he didn't care what anyone thought about him. I loved him so much it rubbed off on me because I was desperate to protect him."

"I think Zander probably protected you when you were younger, too, didn't he?"

Harper nodded. "He's always been loyal."

"And I didn't believe you when I found out," Jared said, his eyes somber as he thought about his initial meeting with the feisty blonde.

"I was just like Josh. I thought Mel was pulling my leg. I thought you were obviously crazy and Whisper Cove was small enough that everyone indulged you because you were too cute to lock up in a nuthouse."

"I don't think you're supposed to say nuthouse," Harper said, rubbing her nose against Jared's cheek and causing him to smile.

"Loony bin?"

"Much better."

Jared blew out a sigh and briefly pressed his eyes shut as he cuddled Harper close. "What about Quinn?"

Harper stilled at the question, surprise washing over her. "What about Quinn?"

"I know you don't like talking about him and I'm okay with that," Jared cautioned. "I worried I was going to be jealous of him for a time, but it turns out I'm not. I actually feel bad for the guy. I am jealous of Zander some of the time, but that's another problem.

"When it came to ghosts, though, did Quinn believe you right away?" he continued. "Did he have faith in you before I did?"

"It's not a competition, Jared," Harper said. "Does it really matter?"

"I'm going to take that as a yes," Jared said, making a face. "I'm sorry I didn't believe you sooner. I feel really badly about doubting you now. I wish I could take it back."

"Jared, you need to understand something about Quinn," Harper said, fidgeting as she licked her lips. "I cared about him, but ... I already feel closer to you than I ever did to him. That might frighten you away, but it's the truth."

"It doesn't frighten me away," Jared said, kissing her ear. "It makes me feel good. I still don't like that he believed you before I did. It makes me feel like an ass."

"He only believed me because he came to town looking for my help to talk to a ghost," Harper pointed out.

Jared narrowed his eyes. He realized he'd never heard the true story behind Harper's romance with Quinn – not that he wanted the gritty details – and he had no idea how they met. "I don't understand."

"Quinn came to me because he wanted to communicate with the

ghost of his sister," Harper explained. "I don't want to go into private details that he wouldn't want spread around, but he was so desperate to find out who killed her he was losing sleep."

"Did you help him?"

"His sister was long gone," Harper replied. "I tried, but ... she was gone. Quinn finally accepted there was nothing he could do and decided to let it go. The next thing I knew he moved to Whisper Cove and asked me out on a date."

"That's ... presumptuous."

"Says the guy who showed up at my office with flowers and candy and kissed me until I relented and forgave him," Harper shot back.

"Yes, well ... we were already technically dating when I did that," Jared said. "Besides, we're talking about him and not me. Everything I do is to be considered cute and charming. Other guys are a different story."

"I hadn't dated anyone in a long time when Quinn showed up," Harper said. "He was nice and attractive. We went out and we were relatively happy."

"Do you still miss him?"

"I guess I should feel guilty for saying no, but I don't," Harper replied. "Before your ego balloons up, I'm not sure I really missed him before you turned my life on its head. I've been used to his absence for a very long time."

"Would you miss me?"

"Oh, I see you're fishing for a compliment," Harper teased.

"I'm just looking for insight," Jared clarified.

"I would miss you terribly," Harper said. "Why do you think I was so angry when you didn't call while you were at your mother's house?"

"I think you like being angry because it gets you going," Jared answered, pressing a soft kiss to her lips. "I'm still sorry about how Josh reacted to this. I honestly thought he would do better."

"You can't force him to accept something he's not ready to accept," Harper said. "He might surprise you if we give him a little bit of time."

"I guess," Jared said, resting his chin on Harper's shoulder. "How long do you think Hal is going to be?"

"I have no idea," Harper answered, glancing at the concentrating ghost. "He's doing the best he can."

The duo lapsed into a comfortable silence that was only interrupted when Josh barreled into the room. "Fine. You're not lying. I accept it and want to help. There. Are you satisfied?"

"This guy is such a boob," Hal said.

EIGHTEEN

"Why do you believe now?" Jared asked, holding Harper steady in her spot as she tried to push herself off of his lap. "Why couldn't you believe before? What changed in the last twenty minutes?"

"Nothing changed," Josh answered. "It's more like ... things slipped into place."

"How so?"

"I saw her outside talking to thin air," Josh supplied. "I assumed she was talking to herself. I realize now she was probably talking to a ghost."

"You assumed I was hiding a secret," Harper pointed out. "What secret were you envisioning?"

"Honestly?"

Harper nodded.

"I thought maybe you were on medicine to curb some mental problems," Josh admitted. "Jared didn't seem worried about you talking to thin air. Even if he was used to it, I figured I would get some sort of reaction out of him and if you were off your meds then he would get you back on them."

"You thought I was off my meds?" Harper wrinkled her nose. "I'm pretty sure I should be insulted."

"Don't worry, Heart," Jared said. "He just wants you to be crazy so he can rationalize you picking me over him. It's an ego thing."

"No, I legitimately thought she might be crazy," Josh said. "I very clearly heard her holding up a one-sided conversation and she was very evasive when I questioned her. You're a terrible liar, by the way, Harper."

"I told you," Jared said, poking Harper's ribs. "You're too sweet and blunt to be a good liar. I knew you were lying to me that night you were searching for Annie's ghost. You put on a good show, but people can tell when you're lying."

Josh knit his eyebrows together. "You arrested Harper for trespassing at a dead woman's house," he said. "She was there to help a ghost. See, all of this stuff is falling into place. Where is Hal? Does he remember where he left his body yet?"

"He's by the map," Harper said, pointing. "He thinks you're a boob."

Jared barked out a laugh while Josh frowned.

"I see this ghost thing is convenient when you're irritated with someone."

"I'm not irritated with you, Josh," Harper said. "I'm … worried … that you're trying to force yourself to an outcome you might not be ready to accept because you're desperate to stay on Jared's good side."

"And what outcome is that?"

"You didn't want to believe I could see ghosts and I understand that," Harper said. "You're not the first non-believer I've met. Jared didn't believe either."

"You didn't?" Josh looked relieved. "What made you believe?"

"Harper made me believe," Jared answered. "She's the most honest person I know."

"That's really sweet and romantic," Josh said.

"It really is," Harper agreed. "It's also complete and total crap."

"Excuse me?" Jared was irritated. "I just said something romantic and honest and you called it crap."

"That's because it is crap," Harper said. "I adore you, Jared, but you did not start believing me because you had faith in me. You were attracted to me and didn't want to be. That forced you to come around more than you initially envisioned.

"You didn't start believing me until I told you where to find Annie's car and that her keys would probably be under the driver's side door," she continued. "Then you were still leery until I told you about the missing iPad. You didn't truly believe until … well … I almost died."

"You almost died?" Josh asked. "How?"

"Harper, I believed you before that night at your house," Jared said quietly. "I can't identify the exact moment I knew, but I believed in you no matter what you might think. You were impossible to doubt."

"That's very sweet, but you're still full of crap," Harper argued.

"I'll show you who is full of crap," Jared grumbled, digging his fingers into Harper's soft flesh as he tickled her and caused her to squeal.

"This relationship is even weirder now that I know the truth," Josh lamented. "How can you deal with this, Jared?"

"Because I don't want to go through life without Harper," Jared replied. "I deal with it because I want her. To be fair, though, it doesn't really bother me. Most people in Whisper Cove know what Harper can do and they're absolutely fine with it."

"Still, though, it's weird."

"Maybe you're weird," Harper suggested.

"He's definitely weird," Hal said, turning away from the map.

"What's the verdict?" Harper asked.

"Is she talking to Hal?" Josh asked.

"Shh." Jared pressed his finger to his mouth to quiet his friend.

"I have no idea where my body is and I'm very upset," Hal said. "I can't remember. I'm sorry."

"That's okay," Harper said. "The truth is your body can't be very far away. The storm has kept everyone inside. Anyone even trying to leave would risk suspicion. Your body is here. It's been hidden. We just need to figure out where."

"There are storage rooms," Josh suggested. "People rarely go inside. I can look in those."

"You should do that," Harper said, pushing herself up from Jared's lap and pacing in front of the map. "I think we need to try something else, Jared."

"And what is that?" Jared asked.

"I'm almost afraid to tell you."

"I'm going to hate this, aren't I?" Jared asked, his shoulders drooping.

"You're definitely going to hate this."

"YOU ARE UNBELIEVABLE," JARED MUTTERED A HALF HOUR later, lowering his raincoat hood and glancing around the tiny mausoleum with mild discomfort. "I cannot believe I let you talk me into going out in this."

"We need help," Harper said. "Hal believes he was murdered. We might get lucky and find out he wasn't murdered and simply freaked out, but that's not usually the case.

"These storms have done something to help us whether you realize it or not," she continued. "They've kept a killer from being able to leave … or discard a body in the lake."

"I never considered that," Jared said, rubbing the back of his neck. "The lake makes an easy place to dump a body. All someone would need is a boat."

"And there are a lot of boats on the island," Harper said. "I checked the weather report about an hour ago. We're going to luck out because another round of storms is coming in tonight. By early tomorrow morning, though, they're going to be out of here … and I'm really worried that means a killer is going to be out of here, too."

"We won't let that happen," Jared said, wiping some of the moisture from Harper's cheek. "We'll figure it out. We need help, though. Can you find your friend?"

"I'm on it," Harper said, rolling to the balls of her feet and giving Jared a quick kiss. "I loved your story about believing in me."

"Don't push me on that," Jared warned. "When this is over with I'm going to push you right back and make you play hopping soap with me until you admit I believed in you long before that night at your house."

"I'm sure I can be persuaded to play," Harper said. "I ... ." She inadvertently jolted when Alice popped into view. "There you are."

"She's here?" Jared asked, relieved. "What is she saying?"

Harper furrowed her brow. "She's not saying anything yet. You need to calm down and give me a chance to ask her some questions."

"Yes, ma'am."

"Thank you," Harper said, plastering what she hoped looked like an innocent smile on her face as she turned back to Alice. For her part, the ghost looked confused more than terrified. "Are you Alice Thorpe?"

The ghost nodded.

"Did you know the Stokes family years ago?"

The ghost nodded again, although this time she seemed sadder.

"Did you die here?" Harper asked.

"Yes." Alice's voice was barely a whisper when she found the strength to speak.

"Thank you for talking," Harper said, taking two baby steps and sitting in the marble chair toward the center of the room. The mausoleum wasn't big, especially by modern standards, but each small area had been set up as something of a showplace. Given what she'd learned about Josh's mother, Harper had to wonder if that was Janet's doing. She made a mental note to ask Josh later. "How long have you been here, Alice?"

"Sometimes it doesn't feel like I've been here long at all," Alice replied. "Other times it feels like I've been here forever."

"I understand that," Harper said. "I know time has no meaning when you're floating. I can help you move to a better place if you're interested. I might need your help first, though."

"And why would you need my help?"

"I'm looking for a body."

Alice dubiously glanced around the mausoleum. "I think you came to the right place."

Harper chuckled and nodded, encouraging Alice to get comfortable as she tried to elicit answers from her. Instead of pushing the situation, Jared made his way over to Harper's side and wordlessly sat on the arm of her chair. He was content letting her do her thing without intruding.

"How did you die, Alice?"

"I was suffocated in my sleep."

Alice was so matter-of-fact Harper thought she must've initially heard the woman wrong. "I'm sorry, what did you say?" Harper asked.

"I was suffocated in my sleep," Alice said. "I remember it quite clearly. One moment I was asleep – I really relished sleep in those days because the baby was colicky and refused to sleep for more than an hour or two in a row – and the next moment I couldn't breathe.

"I didn't realize what was happening until it was too late," she continued. "I fought for a few moments, but the hands ... those awful hands on top of the pillow ... they cut off my air supply early and weakened me. I never really had a shot.

"I think I knew it was coming," she continued. "I kept having dreams about being chased. I could never see the face of the man following me, but I think it was death."

"I'm sorry to hear that," Harper said, meaning every word and swallowing hard. That explained the dream. It was Alice's nightmare and fear manifesting while she slept. It was strong enough to remain behind and infiltrate Harper's head decades after the fact. "I'm sure that was a hard way to go. Do you know who killed you?"

Alice shook her head. "I have an idea, but no proof."

"Who?"

"I would rather not say," Alice said. "It was a long time ago. While I don't know exactly how much time has passed, I know it's been a long time. I've seen the grounds change. I've seen the fashion change. I've seen the house change. It's a hotel now. Nothing is static."

"Did you live in the house?"

"I did," Alice said. "I was the lady of the house."

Harper frowned and glanced at Jared.

"What?" Jared asked, sensing the shift in her mood. "What did she say?"

"She said that she was smothered in her bed by a pillow over her face," Harper replied. "She said she knows a lot of time has passed because the house and grounds have changed. She also says she used to live here."

Jared frowned. "I don't understand," he said. "I'm fairly certain that Josh's father was an only child. That's why it was such a relief when Josh came home. He's an only child, too. He's the only heir. I don't believe there ever was a sister. Maybe Thorpe is her married name, though."

"Are you Linden's sister?" Harper asked.

"No," Alice said, shaking her head. "I'm Linden's wife."

"But ... ." Harper turned back to Jared, her mouth agape. "I'm so confused."

"Now what?"

"She says she's Linden's wife."

"That can't be right," Jared said. "Janet and Linden have been married for decades. She's Josh's mother."

"I'm Josh's mother," Alice clarified.

"What do you mean?" Harper asked, leaning forward. "How can you be Josh's mother?"

"I gave birth to him," Alice replied. "I believe that's how one becomes someone's mother. Didn't your mother explain about the birds and the bees to you?"

"There's no reason to get snippy," Harper chided. "I'm trying to understand. Josh calls Janet his mother. She's been the lady of this house for a very long time. I don't understand how you're Josh's mother when Janet has been pretending to be his mother for most of his life."

"It's not a complicated story really," Alice said, her ethereal fingers busy as they played with a gold chain around her neck. "I married Linden two months after our high school graduation. We were child-hood sweethearts and we were very excited to get married. Janet Marcil was my best friend. She stood up for me at our wedding."

"Oh, well, this sounds like it's going to a creepy place," Harper said, reaching for Jared's hand. He willingly gave it and then sat back and waited for Harper to get all of the information so she could relay it back to him.

"I always knew Janet had a crush on Linden," Alice explained.

"She was very happy for me, though. She was Josh's godmother. She doted on him and loved him like he was her own."

"How much time did you have with Josh before you died?"

"Three months," Alice replied. She pulled her necklace out and revealed a golden locket, just like the one Jared found on the beach. She opened it and showed Harper a photograph of a tiny infant. "They were the best months of my life. I loved that baby."

Harper nodded, her stomach churning. "Did you love Linden?"

"I loved Linden, too," Alice confirmed. "There were times I worried Linden could never love me the way I loved him – his eye wandered at times – but I think he truly loved me when it came down to it. I didn't have a lot of choices once the marriage was proposed by our fathers, so I made do."

"You're saying it was basically an arranged marriage," Harper said, her mind busy.

"Not exactly," Alice clarified. "I loved Linden and chose to date him in high school. I had a feeling we would get married, and I was fine with that. Once we graduated our fathers took over and told us when we would marry. It was a marriage of convenience, but I like to think it was a marriage based on love, too."

"Were you having problems with Linden when you died?"

"I was on top of the world when I died," Alice replied. "I was exhausted but happy. That's why I didn't react to the pillow over my face until it was too late. I couldn't believe anything bad could happen when I was that happy. I tried to fight it … but I was too weak for some reason."

"Did Linden kill you?"

"I don't know who killed me," Alice replied. "I only have an idea who might have killed me. There's a difference. I will not cast aspersions on someone long after my passing ceased to matter."

"You shouldn't say things like that," Harper said. "You're Josh's mother. Your passing means something to him."

"Are you even sure Josh knows I'm his mother?" Alice challenged. "I've seen him throughout the years. He was a handsome boy and he's grown into a fine man. He does not look out here to find his mother, though."

"Well, I don't care," Harper sniffed. "That's not fair. You're his mother and he has a right to know where he came from. You have a right to claim him, too."

"Claiming him is not as important as his happiness."

"And that's why you're his true mother," Harper said, hopping to her feet. "Okay. We've got a lot going on and we have to prioritize. I don't think it's a coincidence we have two ghosts running around the same piece of property."

"You don't?" Jared was flummoxed. "How do you think Alice's murder play's into Hal's?"

"I have no idea yet, but we're going to find out," Harper said, dusting off her hands. "We're all going to have jobs to do, including you, Alice."

"Me? What do you want me to do?"

"There's a body on this parcel of land," Harper explained. "I'm not talking about one of the bodies that belongs in this mausoleum. A man named Hal was killed yesterday – he believes he was murdered, but can't remember how it happened. We can't find his body. I need you to find it."

"Where should I look?"

"Wherever someone would go to hide a body," Harper answered. "We're in the corner room on the east side of the building looking out at the lake. You'll find us there when you discover where the body is."

"Okay," Alice said, unbothered by Harper's bossy attitude. "What are you going to do?"

"I'm going to find out why everyone in this family has been covering up your existence for thirty years," Harper said. "There has to be a reason, and when we find that reason we'll probably be able to put all of the past pieces and current pieces together to solve the Stokes family's ultimate jigsaw puzzle."

"I love it when you get feisty and motivated," Jared said, grinning. "I would hate to be the person standing between you and your answers when this is all said and done."

"Me, too."

NINETEEN

"I don't understand any of this," Jared said forty minutes later, pulling his shirt over his head and tossing it on the floor in front of the bathroom. Despite his best efforts to cover himself with a rain slicker, the storm remnants were strong and he was soaked to the bone. "Why would the Stokes cover up Alice's death?"

"Forget covering up her death. They covered up her entire existence," Harper said, appearing in the space between the bathroom and bedroom wearing nothing but her panties and bra. "Why would Linden erase his wife's memory?"

"I ... um ... what did you say?" Jared lost his train of thought as he looked Harper up and down. Her hair was wet and snarled from the elements. Her eye makeup ran down her face. She was still beautiful, and he couldn't stop his mind from wandering when he saw her.

"Are you even listening to me?"

"Honestly? I can't when you look like that," Jared admitted sheepishly. "I keep having flashbacks to when I was sixteen and was desperate to see a girl in her underwear. If grown-up me could go back and whisper something in the ear of teenage me it would be not to worry because it's going to happen, and it's going to be marvelous."

"Ha, ha," Harper intoned, although she couldn't help but laugh at Jared's honesty and self-deprecating humor. "You're good for my ego."

"You're good for my everything," Jared said. "Come here."

"No way," Harper said, dodging his hands when he reached for her. "If we touch one another right now we're going to lose the whole afternoon."

"You say that like it's a bad thing." Jared reached for Harper's narrow waist again, but she was expecting the move and easily side-stepped him.

"We have serious things to discuss," Harper said. "We have a dead body somewhere in this house."

"I know," Jared said. "It's terrible. If you don't stop running from me, though, I'm going to have to wrestle you down and no one wants that. Well, wait, I might want that."

"Jared, we have to talk about serious things."

"I know we do, Harper," Jared said, his face full of faux concern. "I just need to do one other thing first."

"Fine," Harper said. "Once we're done, though, I'm in charge and I'm going to mean business."

"Good," Jared said, his hand already at Harper's hip. "I love it when you use your stern face."

"WHAT ARE YOU DOING?" JARED MURMURED A HALF HOUR later, refusing to open his eyes as he cuddled behind Harper. "You need to take a nap with me."

"I can't take a nap," Harper replied. "There's too much going on. We've already lost too much time."

"Shh," Jared said, blindly kissing her cheek. "You're sleepy. You want me to hold you so we can take a nap and then figure out what to do over dinner. You're very sleepy and need rest. Shh."

"I can't take a nap when I need information," Harper countered. "Go to sleep. I'll handle everything we need and then I'll join you."

"Something tells me that's not going to happen," Jared said, although he couldn't force his eyes open to see what Harper worked on with her cell phone as he draped an arm over her hip. "I need you to sleep with me."

"Just give me five minutes to text Zander a few instructions and I'll be right with you. I promise."

THE NEXT TIME JARED WOKE HE WAS MORE AWARE OF HIS surroundings. He had no idea what wore him out so completely before – other than spending quality time with Harper – but he was aware and ready to take on the day when his eyes popped open about two hours before dinner.

Unfortunately for him, Harper was now dead to the world. Jared smiled as he looked her over, carefully taking the cell phone clutched in her hand and jolting when Zander's face appeared in the window.

"What are you doing?" Zander asked.

"What are you doing?" Jared shot back. "Were you sitting on Skype waiting for her to wake up?"

"Is she asleep?"

Jared moved the phone so Zander could get a gander at his drooling best friend. He was laughing when Jared pulled the phone back up to his chest.

"She's going to kill you when she finds out you did that," Zander said. Jared couldn't help but notice that Zander was purposely keeping his voice low so he wouldn't wake Harper. "I'm going to laugh so hard next time I talk to her."

"You didn't answer my question," Jared prodded. "Were you waiting for Harper to wake up so you could talk to her?"

"You happened to pick up at the exact same moment I placed a call," Zander replied. "I thought it was on purpose."

"It was an accident," Jared said. "I didn't want to wake her, but I was curious what she was working on while I slept. I have no idea why I was so exhausted, but I couldn't keep my eyes open."

"It was a heady mixture of rain, sex, and heat," Zander supplied. "That's what Harper and I decided while you were asleep anyway."

"I see," Jared said, tamping down his irritation. He found that he missed Zander, and it was a surprising revelation. That didn't mean the man didn't irritate him, or that he wouldn't enjoy a bit more privacy when the three of them were together under the same roof. "What did she have you looking up?"

"Oh, she wanted to see what kind of information I could get on Alice Thorpe," Zander said.

Things clicked into place for Jared. "Did you find anything? This whole situation is weird and she's obsessed with finding out why no one talks about Alice."

"This whole situation *is* weird," Zander agreed, leaning back in his desk chair. "I wasn't sure where to look so I called for help."

"Who?" Jared asked, genuinely confused. "Is Eric there? You're not letting him see Harper drooling in her sleep, are you? She won't like that. She's going to be ticked off enough that you saw her."

"It's not Eric," Zander answered, smiling as his uncle Mel pushed himself into the frame. "I need someone who could look at old police records and my options were limited."

"Oh," Jared said, fighting the urge to laugh when he saw his partner. "Hi, Mel. How are you?"

"How are you?" Mel asked. "I hear things aren't going great for you on your vacation. I'm sorry. I know you were looking forward to having time alone with Harper without this one bothering you." He affectionately tousled Zander's hair. "It sounds like you might have trouble."

"We might," Jared confirmed. "The problem is that I won't know if we have trouble until we find a body and we can't find a body without help from ghosts."

Mel made a face. He waffled on whether or not he believed Harper could see and talk to ghosts. He was convinced she was special. It was the ghost aspects that threw him from time to time.

"Harper provided us with names to run. Which one do you want first?" Mel asked.

"Hal Baker," Jared sad, rubbing his thumb up and down Harper's bare arm as she blissfully slumbered. "He's the one who is missing and presumed dead. He has to be our focus."

"Hal Baker is sixty-one years old," Mel supplied. "He has ties to this area, although they're kind of muddy. He went to high school in Harbor Beach, which is up in the thumb but not terribly far away."

"You're saying he was familiar with Harsens Island?" Jared asked.

"We can't prove that," Mel cautioned. "He was familiar with Michigan. We can't put him on Harsens Island specifically."

"Still, it seems like too much of a coincidence to ignore," Jared said. "One of the other mystery actors said that Hal was offended because he was put in a room in the basement. The level used to be quarters for the help a really long time ago, but when they turned the house into a hotel they upgraded those rooms."

"Is that Cara?" Zander asked, making a face.

"How did you know that?"

"Because Harper didn't like how she was throwing herself at you," Zander said. "You were out like a light so you missed that part of our conversation."

"Harper has nothing to be jealous about," Jared said. "She should know that. I told Cara I was happy with my blonde."

"I know," Zander said. "Harper was almost giddy when she told me that part of the conversation. Sometimes I forget she's still a girl and can't help herself from reacting to things like a normal woman."

Jared rolled his eyes and shook his head. "Harper has nothing to worry about. Do not fan any flames about stuff like this. I don't like it."

"You should like it," Zander argued. "Harper is basically telling you she's jealous and wants you. This is the girl version of 'marking your territory.' It's the same thing you do when you put your hand on her waist when another guy approaches Harper to talk to her.

"You're saying she's yours," he continued. "Harper being jealous is saying the same thing, just in a girly way."

"I'm not sure I followed that," Mel said.

"I'm pretty sure you don't want to follow it," Jared said. "Go back to Hal. What are his financials like?"

"I wouldn't say they're dire, but he's not exactly rolling in dough," Mel replied. "I don't think there's a lot of money in murder mystery troupes. He does okay, but he doesn't own a home and he basically lives in a crappy rental in Ohio during his off time, which isn't much because he's constantly working."

"Does he have any enemies you can find?"

"Not really," Mel said. "He doesn't have ties to anyone because he's always moving around. I guess you could say he has ties to members of the mystery troupe, but he's the only long-term holdout. The turnover in that group is pretty high."

"I'm guessing it's because everyone thinks the mystery troupe is a stepping stone to greatness," Jared said. "Cara thinks she's going to be a big actress and she suggested I hop on her before that happens because I would regret it afterward."

"And what do you think?" Mel asked.

"I think the only thing I would regret is losing Harper," Jared said, his fingers drifting over the graceful curve of Harper's neck. "What about Alice Thorpe?"

"Alice is another story," Mel said. "Information on her is tight. I don't think it helps that she died before the Internet was big, but it seems something else might be going on here."

"Like?"

"Like maybe the Stokes family paid money to lock her records up," Mel supplied. "There's no digital information on her other than a few cursory things. We have a date of birth and death. We have a marriage certificate. We have a death certificate. That's about it."

"What does the death certificate say?"

"She died of a heart attack in her sleep," Mel answered.

"How old was she?"

"Twenty-Nine."

"She died of a heart attack in her sleep when she was twenty-nine?" Jared asked, incredulous. "That seems highly unlikely, especially since she told Harper she was suffocated in her sleep not long after she gave birth to Josh."

"I can't speak for the investigators because they're all long gone," Mel said. "There might have been a cover up. There might not have been a cover up. We simply don't know and I'm not sure how we could get that information even if it's out there to claim."

"Have Harper talk to Alice again," Zander suggested. "She said

Alice had an idea who killed her but wouldn't say who it was. My money is on the husband. It's always the husband."

"In theory, that's a possibility," Jared said. "I've known Linden a number of years, though, and I've never considered him as someone who would be capable of murder. You also have the second wife, who I always thought was the only wife, and she's extremely unpleasant.

"Alice told Harper that Janet was her best friend and Josh's godmother," he continued. "Josh made it sound as if he's never gotten along with his mother and things have gotten out of hand recently because of the financial problems. What if Janet killed Alice because she wanted a slice of the Stokes financial pie?"

"If that's the case, do you think she's capable of killing Josh if he stands in her way of spending money?" Mel asked.

"I honestly don't know," Jared said. "There's a lot to consider here and we only have an hour and a half before dinner. Keep looking and see what you can find. I need to wake up Sleeping Beauty and get her in the shower. We have a lot to deal with over the next few hours and we're going to have to come up with a game plan."

"You need to be careful," Mel said. "You're cut off and the police presence on Harsens Island is minimal. Even if you could get help, the Stokes family is like royalty out there. There's a chance the local boys might not be willing to help."

"We'll keep our eyes open and be in touch," Jared said. "If you find any information, email it to us. Don't call us unless it's really important. We're going to be following people around and feeling them out tonight. An ill-timed phone call might cause problems."

"You're saying that for my benefit, right?" Zander asked.

Jared smirked. "Do you know what? I was just thinking when I answered the phone that I actually missed you. I have no idea how long that will last – and not long if your attitude stays like this – but I actually miss you."

"Of course you do," Zander said. "I make everyone's life richer and fun."

"Especially Harper's," Jared said. "I know she misses you, too, even if she won't admit it because she thinks it would bother me."

"Give Harper a kiss for me, but not a filthy one," Zander said.

"We'll keep digging. It sounds like things are going to come to a head there no matter what."

"I don't see any other way around it," Jared said. "Hal is dead on this property somewhere. The house is huge, but we can't let these people go until we know how he died and who killed him if he was murdered."

"What about Alice's murder?" Mel asked. "What are you going to do about that?"

"I'm not sure there's anything we can do," Jared replied. "We can't take the word of a ghost to a judge for a warrant, that's for sure. I'll talk to Josh, but … I honestly don't know if he realizes Janet isn't his mother."

"If he doesn't, his father certainly did him a disservice," Mel said. "There's no reason Josh couldn't love Janet like a second mother. He deserved to know about his real mother, though."

"I agree," Jared said. "See if you can find anything. In fact, go to Phil. Ask him about Linden. Linden knew Harper's grandfather and he mentioned going to summer camp with Phil. It's a long shot, but Phil might know some dirt on the family."

"I'm on it," Zander said. "We'll figure this out. Don't worry."

"I'm not worried."

"Oh, and Jared?"

Jared stilled with his hand close to the disconnect button. "Yeah?"

"I miss you, too."

TWENTY

"How do you want to handle this?" Harper asked an hour and a half later, slipping her hand into Jared's and letting him lead her into the dining room. "Are you just going to blurt out that Janet isn't his mother and then hope Josh's isn't upset?"

"No," Jared said, leading Harper toward their usual table. "I'm going to play it by ear."

"That's your plan?" Harper wasn't impressed.

"Do you have a better suggestion?" Jared asked, pulling Harper's chair out and making sure she was settled before planting a soft kiss on her cheek and moving to the chair next to her. "I don't want to play games, but I'm not sure how Josh is going to take this on top of everything else."

"You're worried he's going to have a meltdown because I said I could see ghosts and now I'm claiming to have talked to his mother – who he didn't realize was his mother – which means his life will be upended."

"I'm not sure what you just said there, but I think that's pretty much right," Jared said. "I want to see how Josh is handling the first bit of jarring news before I launch a second batch in his direction."

"That sounds like a good idea to me," Harper said, grabbing the menu from the center of the table. "Ooh, yum, they have surf and turf again. I love steak and lobster."

Jared chuckled. "Do you know that one of my favorite things about you is your appetite?"

Harper stilled, surprised. "Is that a good thing?"

"It's a very good thing," Jared confirmed. "Other than our first date when you were exceedingly nervous and were going to order a salad, you've never once looked at a meal and thought you shouldn't eat it because you wanted to impress me."

"Would me not eating impress you?"

"No. It would make me sad."

"Then it seems like a moot point," Harper said, reaching for a breadstick. "Do you wish I would eat less? Do you wish I was a dainty girl with a tiny appetite?"

"Absolutely not," Jared answered. "You're naturally thin and you spend half of your time running around with Zander to work off whatever you eat. I think you're beautiful just the way you are. I wouldn't change one thing about you."

"You're being charming tonight," Harper said. "Does that mean you want another bath?"

Jared shrugged. "I would like to take another look at the case of the hopping soap," he said, grinning. "We have other things to consider first, though."

"Like talking to Josh," Harper said.

"Like talking to Josh."

"Like talking to Josh about what?" Josh took Harper and Jared by surprise when he appeared at the edge of the table. "Where have you guys been all day?"

"We've been multiple places," Jared answered, recovering quickly and gesturing toward the chair across from him. "Have a seat."

"I don't like the sound of that," Josh said, although he did as instructed. "Did you guys find anything interesting when you took off into the storm? I still think that was crazy, by the way."

"There's a lot to discuss," Jared said, choosing his words carefully. "First off, did you know Hal Baker had ties to Michigan?"

"No," Josh replied. "Is there a reason I should know that?"

"He grew up in Harbor Beach, and while that could be a coincidence, I learned a long time ago that most coincidences are something else entirely," Jared said. "We can't specifically tie Hal to Harsens Island yet, but my partner is looking into his background."

"Why is that important?" Josh asked.

"Because we need to know where he's been if we want to figure out where he is now," Jared explained. "He can't seem to remember what happened to his body. I'm starting to wonder if it's not that he can't remember as much as he doesn't want to remember."

"I don't know what that means," Josh said. "Are you saying he's a liar?"

"He could very well be," Jared confirmed.

"This day just keeps getting freakier and freakier," Josh lamented.

"If Hal is lying, there has to be a reason why he's pretending not to know what happened to him," Jared said. "He seemed angry when Harper discovered him in the library, but it was more like he was angry that no one noticed he was dead than anything else."

"He has delusions of grandeur," Harper said. "I think that's his biggest problem. He thinks he should be something that he's not."

"Which is?" Josh pressed.

"If I had to guess, I think his biggest problem is that he's not famous and he's been marginalized in the minds of others and maybe even himself," Harper said. "He probably had dreams of moving on to bigger and better things at one point – like Jared's flirty friend Cara and her fake boobs – and that dream slipped away a long time ago. That made him bitter."

"I heard you told Zander about Cara, by the way," Jared said, momentarily changing the subject and taking Harper by surprise. "I had no idea that bothered you so much. Zander claims that your jealousy is the same thing as when I go up to you and put my hand on your waist at a social gathering. It's like marking your territory. Do you believe that?"

"Not really," Harper replied dryly. "I'm not jealous, though, so this entire conversation is conjecture."

"You're not jealous?"

"Not even remotely."

"Guys, as cute as this little foreplay game you're playing is, I'm dying to know what Hal's lies might mean in the grand scheme of things," Josh interjected, his gaze bouncing between Harper and Jared. "I'm glad you like verbally copulating – and that *is* what you were doing, whether you realize it or not – but there may very well be a dead body in my hotel."

Harper glanced around to make sure no one overheard Josh's pronouncement and then turned her attention back to Josh. "I'm sorry. You're right. We shouldn't be focused on our stuff when you have so much going on."

"It's fine," Josh said, waving off Harper's apology. "I just ... ." He didn't get a chance to finish his sentence because the waitress picked that moment to arrive and take their orders. After requesting three surf and turfs and a few drinks, the threesome returned to their conversation once they were alone. "I'm worried that finding a dead body here during a murder mystery could spell the end of this place before it has a chance to really take off."

"You're really worried about losing the house, aren't you?" Jared asked.

"I love this house," Josh answered. "I really do. I spent my childhood here. If we were to lose it, though, strictly from a personal standpoint, I would be okay. I think even my father would be okay. My mother, though, she is a different story. If we lose this house, I'm afraid it will kill her."

Harper and Jared exchanged a look. They had their opening. Now they just had to take it.

"I don't really know a lot about your mother," Jared said, choosing his words carefully as he leaned back in his chair. He was trying to give the appearance of calm ease even though his nerves were tightly coiled. "Did she grow up in this area?"

"She did," Josh confirmed, his gaze busily scanning the packed dining room. He didn't notice the change in Jared's demeanor, which was probably a good thing. "She was born right here on Harsens Island."

"Did she know your father well before they started dating?"

Harper asked. "I would imagine that the island is so small they couldn't help but notice each other."

"I think they were high school sweethearts or something," Josh said. "It's hard for me to remember, mostly because I can't look at their relationship now and reconcile all of the stories I heard as a kid. According to the stories they were like Cinderella and Prince Charming. According to reality, they were more like Ike and Tina Turner – without the beatings, of course. It makes me sad to think they lost the happiness they had when they were prom king and queen and now they have nothing but unhappiness."

Harper licked her lips. She was personally offended on Alice's behalf. Those were her stories and Janet stole them for her own life. Even worse than the stories, though, she stole Alice's son, too. "Do you think your mother always dreamed of living in this house?"

"What do you mean?" Josh asked, confused. "Are you asking if she set out to trap my father or something?"

That was exactly what Harper was asking, but she didn't want Josh to know that. "No," she said, shaking her head. "Of course not. I used to dream about this house and I didn't even live on Harsens Island. I imagine most of the girls in town dreamed about living here."

"Oh, I suppose that makes sense," Josh said. "She's never really talked about anything like that with me, though. In fact, I can't remember any conversation we've shared that's lasted more than five minutes since I hit puberty. Even then, when I started dating, her idea of having a talk was warning me to make sure I wore a condom because she wasn't taking care of any little accident should I screw up."

The admission made Harper inexplicably sad. "I'm really sorry to hear that," she said. "My mother drives me crazy, but she always wants to talk to me no matter what … and talk … and talk … and talk."

"It's never been any different for my mother and me," Josh explained. "I don't know any different so I can't expect anything different. Does that make sense?"

"Not really," Harper said, her heart rolling. "Josh, are you sure the name Alice Thorpe doesn't mean anything to you?"

Josh knit his eyebrows together, confused. "Should it? Is that the name from the photograph in the dining room again?"

Harper nodded.

"I swear I've never heard it before," Josh said. "Why does it matter?"

"Um … ." Harper had no idea how to respond.

"Josh, we've found out a few things since we separated from you this afternoon," Jared said, his voice soft and gentle. "I'm assuming you didn't find anything when you searched the storage rooms, by the way."

"I would've told you if I had," Josh said, his frustration evident. "Tell me what's going on. Other than my initial reaction to Harper's announcement, I think I've been a darned good sport about all of this. I don't like the thought of you guys keeping stuff from me."

"We're not keeping stuff from you," Jared clarified. "It's just … what we have to tell you is going to be difficult and I'm not sure that you're ready to hear it given the rough day you've already had. We don't have a lot of choice in the matter, though."

"And Alice has a right to be remembered," Harper chimed in.

"And Alice is the ghost you were talking to by the road when the storm hit, right?" Josh asked. "You said you were going to help her once the storm cleared. Is that where you two disappeared today? Did you find Alice?"

"We needed to find Alice because we needed help," Harper supplied. "Even though Hal says he can't remember where his body is, I have trouble believing he's telling us the whole truth. Some ghosts don't remember everything about their deaths and that's actually pretty normal. That makes them belligerent and needy, though. Hal is going out of his way to help and coming up with absolutely nothing. That feels somehow wrong to me."

"Okay," Josh said. "What do you think is going on?"

"We found Alice down in one of the mausoleums," Harper said. "She was laid to rest there about thirty years ago."

"That would mean she's a relative," Josh said. "I don't remember any relatives with the last name Thorpe."

"That's because she was going by her married name at the time of her death," Jared interjected quietly.

"And what was her married name?"

"Stokes."

Josh was confused. "Are you saying she's some distant relative of mine and she died on the property? I guess that's not out of the realm of possibility, but I was under the impression that only certain people were buried in the mausoleums. There's limited space so you had to be a full family member to get a spot."

"I don't think he's getting what I'm trying to say," Jared said, rubbing the back of his neck as he searched for the right way to tell Josh the truth.

"Janet isn't your mother," Harper announced. "Alice Thorpe was your mother. She died in her sleep. The death certificate says she had a heart attack, but she was really smothered. Janet was her best friend and somehow she ended up married to your father in the aftermath of your mother's death, but she's not your real mother."

Josh's mouth dropped open as Harper's words washed over him. "W-what?"

"Nice job, Heart," Jared chided, making a face. "You have zero tact sometimes. You're very sweet most of the time, but other times you completely lose your head. What were you thinking?"

"I was thinking that Josh has a right to know who his mother is."

"There was still a better way to tell him," Jared said, turning his sympathetic eyes toward Josh. "Are you okay?"

"That's not true, right?" Josh asked. "What she just told me, that's a lie ... or a game ... or something other than the truth."

"It's the truth," Jared countered. "I don't know everything that is going on, but I do know that Alice Thorpe was married to Linden Stokes. The marriage lasted almost ten years. Right after your birth, Alice was found dead in her bed. It was ruled a heart attack, but ... ."

"But she was murdered," Josh finished, rubbing his chin as the words sank in. "How is this possible?"

"Are you sure your father never hinted around that Janet wasn't your mother?" Harper asked, her heart going out to Josh. "Maybe he said something that didn't jump out at you at the time but now in hindsight it makes you wonder if he was trying to tell you something."

"My father has always been warm and loving toward me," Josh said. "He's never lied to me. Even when we were in real financial trouble and he was embarrassed, he never lied to me. Why would he do this? Why would he lie about this?"

"Maybe he was upset himself," Harper suggested. "Alice said she and Linden were high school sweethearts and very much in love. She said Janet was her best friend and had … um … jealousy issues. She was also your godmother."

"That sounds like the history I heard for my mother … I mean Janet," Josh said, his face pale. "Are you saying that my real mother is dead and Janet stole her story and pretended it was her story?"

Josh looked enraged.

"I'm saying that something very bad happened to Alice and we need to figure out what it was," Harper clarified. "I also think that Hal's death plays into what happened to Alice, although I have no idea how."

"We need to get answers about Alice," Jared prodded. "Who do you think would be the best one to ask?"

"I know exactly who we're going to ask," Josh said, reaching into his pocket so he could retrieve his cell phone. "He can't hide from me forever. It's time I got the truth. He owes me the whole story about my mother at the very least. It's time he told me about her."

TWENTY-ONE

L inden didn't appear worried as he cut a path through the dining room and moved in his son's direction. Josh was terse on the phone but held things together long enough to ask his father to join him for dinner. Once he disconnected he turned into a sweating mess and Harper and Jared spent the intervening five minutes trying to convince him everything was going to be okay.

Linden approached the table with wary eyes. He offered a few of the guests head nods and waves, but never veered from the path he picked. He greeted everyone at the table with a watery smile and then sat, steepling his fingers as he waited for Josh to make his intentions known.

"What's wrong?" Linden asked finally, unable to take another moment of silence.

"What makes you think anything is wrong?" Jared asked, his hand resting on top of Harper's.

"Because Josh is obviously upset and you two look as if you'd rather be in front of a firing squad than me right now," Linden answered. "I'm not an idiot. Talk."

"I have to ask you something," Josh said, licking his lips. "It's a hard question, and I'm worried it's going to upset you … or take you by surprise … or make you really angry. I have to know, though."

"Okay," Linden said. "I'm sure we can get through whatever you need to ask me. Spit it out."

"I … ." Josh was floundering.

"He wants to know about Alice Thorpe," Harper interjected. "He knows she was his mother and Janet's not. He's kind of ticked off and really scared, but I think part of him is also excited because he really doesn't like Janet and she's mean to him."

"Oh, my." Linden exhaled heavily while Josh slapped his hands over his eyes in an attempt to block out the scene.

"You have to stop doing that, Harper," Jared chided. "It's weird and it throws people for a loop."

"Listen, I'm all for being prim, proper, and polite when the conversation warrants it, but we have a lot going on right now and we don't have time to pussyfoot around the bigger issues at play here," Harper said. "We need Linden to admit the truth about Alice so we can move on to the other stuff."

"Thank you, Heart," Jared said, squeezing her hand and shaking his head. "Sometimes I think you channel Zander when it comes to tact."

"I take it you're the ones who told Josh this … story?" Linden asked, his face unreadable.

"We are," Jared confirmed, refusing to back down.

"And how did you hear it?"

"We … um … ."

"I can see and talk to ghosts," Harper offered, her tone blasé even though Jared shot her an incredulous look. "What? I'm not going to lie any longer when we've got so much going on. You were the one who told me to tell the truth from the beginning. This should make you happy"

"You're a piece of work sometimes," Jared grumbled.

"Right back at you."

Linden shook his head as he studied Harper, his usually kind eyes keen. "You can see and talk to ghosts?"

"I know you probably don't believe me, but yes," Harper answered.

"My grandfather was the first one I ever saw, in fact. He came into my room to say goodbye the night he died."

"I guess that makes sense," Linden said.

"You're handling this a lot better than I did a few hours ago," Josh said. "When Harper told me, I accused her of playing an elaborate prank on me and then forced them to storm out and desert me until I came to my senses."

"This isn't the first time I've heard about Harper's abilities," Linden said.

Harper tilted her head to the side, surprised. "Really? Who told you?"

"You're relatively famous in certain circles, Harper," Linden said. "You've found bodies, missing children, and kidnap victims over the course of your short life. People have whispered about you for ages.

"Harsens Island and Whisper Cove are separate, but not by much," he continued. "I heard stories about you and then I ran into your father a few years ago and he confirmed them. He's very proud of you."

"He is?" Harper wrinkled her nose. "I know my father loves me, but he's never seemed especially proud of me."

"That's because you're his only child and he doesn't want to risk crowding you," Linden replied. "I'm the father of one child, too. I know how that works."

"So, wait, you believe her?" Jared asked.

Linden nodded. "I do believe her."

"Is she telling the truth about Alice Thorpe?" Josh asked quietly. "Was she my mother?"

For a second Harper was convinced Linden was going to lie to his son. He didn't.

"She was your mother," Linden confirmed.

Josh let out a strangled gasp and dropped his head in hands. Jared reached out and awkwardly patted him on the shoulder.

"Why didn't you tell Josh about his mother?" Harper asked, taking control of the conversation. "He deserved the right to know about her."

"He did," Linden agreed. "You have to understand, I loved Alice a great deal. I loved her when I was fourteen years old and I loved her when I was thirty. I thought we were going to be together forever. When she died in her sleep at such a young age ... well ... I was lost."

Harper opened her mouth to point out Alice didn't die in her sleep, but Jared offered a small shake of his head to warn her off. Harper read between the lines: Jared wanted Linden to tell the story in his own time.

"I didn't think I would ever get over Alice's death," Linden said. "I was crushed and broken. I didn't get out of bed for days and finally Trask is the one who made me get up for her funeral. I know you don't understand why I keep him on given his attitude, but he was the best friend I had in the dark days after your mother died. I owed him.

"I wasn't a very good father to you during that time, Josh," Linden said. "I was a terrible father, in fact. I had no idea who was taking care of you because I was too busy feeling sorry for myself. I thought I was going to get a full life with Alice. I felt cheated and I was angry."

"That doesn't explain how you ended up with Janet," Harper said, making a face when Jared shot her a dark look. "What? I'm not being a busybody. I'm genuinely curious."

Despite the surreal nature of the situation, Linden chuckled. "She's fine, Jared. I find her refreshing. In fact, I think the reason I took such a shine to her right from the beginning was because she reminded me of my Alice."

Josh made a face. "Are you saying I was attracted to a woman who reminds you of my mother?"

"That's exactly what he's saying so you need to stop hitting on her," Jared said. He wasn't actually trying to be a pain. He was going for levity, though, and they all needed it. "If you keep hitting on her it will be like incest and no one wants that."

"That's pretty convenient for you," Josh quipped. "I guess this whole fake mother thing worked out to your advantage."

"Hey, I think you won here, too," Jared said. "You always wondered why your mother – er, Janet – never bonded with you. Now you know."

"Tell us about Janet," Harper prodded. "I'm dying to understand how Alice's best friend ended up in your bed."

"There's no need to get crude," Linden chided, although his eyes momentarily sparkled. "The truth is, I was at a loss as to what I should be doing following Alice's death. We had plans to add to our family down the road. We wanted three children. We had everything planned out."

"And then she died," Jared supplied.

"And then she died and everything changed," Linden said. "They say you go through stages of grief. I got mired in the anger one a little too long. I became angry at Alice for leaving me alone and I did some absolutely moronic things."

"Like marrying Janet?" Harper asked.

"I know it might seem hard to believe now given the stories you've probably heard about Janet, but she was a good woman at one time," Linden said. "She's the one who took care of Josh when I was inconsolable after Alice's death. She made sure he was fed and loved. She rocked him to sleep every night. She loved him. Of course, she was his godmother, she had to love him."

"How did all of that change?" Josh asked. "How did she grow to hate me?"

"She doesn't hate you, Josh," Linden clarified. "She's simply ... limited. I didn't realize it at the time because I was paralyzed with grief, but Janet has emotional deficits. She can't engage with people. I wasn't engaging with people when I decided to marry her, and it was far too late to change things once I realized what was going on."

"You married Janet because you didn't know what else to do, didn't you?" Jared asked.

Linden nodded. "I didn't believe it was possible to love anyone ever again and Josh needed a mother," he said. "I knew Janet had a crush on me. Alice and I used to laugh about it when we were alone sometimes. I thought Janet would jump at the chance to live in the house and take care of Josh. I thought that would be enough."

"When did you realize it wasn't enough?" Harper asked.

"I lived that first year in a fog," Linden answered. "I did my best to spend time with Josh, although it wasn't quality time. I managed to get my act together better on that as time passed, but that first year I was neglectful and I've always felt guilty about it."

"It's not like I remember it," Josh pointed out. "You were in mourning."

"I was in mourning, but I should've done almost everything differently," Linden said. "If I had things to do over again ... ."

"You can't go back in time," Harper said. "What happened with Janet?"

"Janet thought I married her out of love and then slowly came to the realization that I married her out of convenience," Linden replied. "For a time I think she believed she could change my mind and make me fall in love with her. She doted on me ... and Josh ... and she went out of her way to be a loving wife and mother.

"At some point realization kicked in because she grew bitter," he continued. "I'm not sure when it happened. One day I looked at her and realized it wasn't love I was seeing reflected back in her eyes but hate."

"Why did you keep Alice's memory hidden?" Harper asked. "That doesn't seem fair to her, especially because you claim that you loved her."

"I was angry with her for a very long time," Linden said. "I didn't know how to grieve properly so I blamed her for something she had no control over. When Josh started asking questions as a child I decided it would be easier for him if he believed Janet was his mother. It's not like Alice's family ever came to visit. He didn't know any of his relatives on that side of the family. After Alice died they ceased visiting. I thought it would be better for Josh if he thought Janet was his mother. I didn't want him spending his adolescence searching for a ghost."

"That's kind of ironic when you think about it," Harper muttered.

"By the time Josh hit middle school I realized I made a mistake," Linden said. "I approached Janet, intent on telling Josh the truth and hoping we could do it as a unit, but she had a complete and total meltdown. She said that she was Josh's mother and she wouldn't stand for any talk of Alice in her house. That's when I realized how much Janet had changed.

"I know it sounds simplistic, or even asinine, but I was oblivious to many of Janet's faults until it was too late to fix what I had done," he continued. "Josh has turned into a happy and well-adjusted adult. I thought he deserved to know about his mother, but I didn't want to rock the boat. That's on me."

"Harper showed me her photograph in the dining room," Josh said. "If Mom … I mean Janet … wanted my real mother out of this house so badly, why did she leave the photo up?"

"I don't know," Linden answered. "You'll have to ask her that. She went through a period where she scoured through the entire house to make sure nothing of Alice's remained. I regret that."

"That must be how Alice's locket ended up in the water," Harper said. "We found it there the other day. I recognized it when her ghost showed me her locket today."

Josh looked hopeful. "Really?"

"It's in our room," Harper said, sympathy rolling off of her. "We'll make sure you get it. You're going to have to take it to a jeweler to get it open, but … you'll have something from your real mother."

"We have another problem," Jared added. "Actually, we have several other problems. The first is that Alice is still hanging around and needs to be put to rest. She's been walking these grounds for thirty years. I think she deserves some peace."

"How was I supposed to know that?" Linden asked.

"You weren't," Harper said. "The thing is, um, most souls don't hang around because they died in their sleep. They hang around because they were murdered."

Linden stilled, surprised. "No. That's not right. Alice went to sleep and never woke up. We had a doctor come out here and everything."

"I don't want to upset you, but the odds of a woman as young as Alice dying in her sleep aren't very good," Jared said. "My partner has been going over Alice's records, and he says it's almost as if there's been a concerted effort to wipe Alice from the record books."

"Is that possible?" Josh asked. "This is the information age. You can't erase people now."

"Alice died long before the information age," Jared replied. "She also claims she was suffocated in her sleep."

"What?" Linden's eyebrows flew up his forehead. "You can't be serious."

"She was pretty convincing," Harper said. "She said she felt exhausted and that's why she didn't wake up, but I'm going to bet if we did an autopsy we would find she'd been drugged to make it easier for someone to suffocate her."

"Does she know who killed her?" Josh asked.

"If she does, she's not saying," Harper said. "She's ... complicated. I think she's bitter about her memory being erased from the house, but she called Josh handsome and a good man."

"She's seen me?" Josh looked hopeful.

"She's seen everything," Harper said. "In fact, I have her out looking for Hal's body right now. If we're lucky she'll be able to find it and help us solve our second mystery."

"Wait a second," Linden said. "Who is Hal?"

"That's what I was just about to ask you," Jared said. "Hal Baker is the head of the mystery troupe. He's dead. Harper ran into his ghost in the library. He's playing coy and says he doesn't know where his body is, but something else is going on and Harper is convinced all of this – Alice's murder and Hal's death – somehow all play together."

"How is that even possible?" Linden asked. "Alice died more than two decades ago."

"I want to see everything you have of hers, by the way," Josh said. "I want to see it all."

"You can have everything I've managed to hide away," Linden said, patting his son's hand. "I'm sorry I kept it from you. I will be forever thankful you had help finding the truth, though. It's a relief not to have to lie."

"Hal Baker has ties to Harbor Beach," Jared said. "I don't think that's a coincidence. I think having two ghosts on the same property means something ... although I have no idea what."

"I don't know any Hal Baker," Linden said. "That name means absolutely nothing to me. I don't even remember him from the game."

"Here," Josh said, pulling his phone out of his pocket and flipping through a few photos. "That's him without his makeup."

Linden took the phone and studied it, furrowing his brow as he looked at the photograph from three different angles. "That's Hal Baker?"

Jared nodded. "Why? Do you recognize him?"

"I definitely recognize him," Linden answered. "I had no idea his name was Hal Baker, though. I knew him by a different name and had no idea he was in this house. If I knew he was here, I would've kicked him out."

"What name did you know him by?"

"Hal Daniels," Linden said. "I didn't recognize him because the only times I saw this guy since he got here he's been in makeup. That's Hal Daniels, though."

"Why does that name sound familiar?" Harper asked.

"Because he's Trask Daniels' brother," Linden answered.

"Oh," Jared and Harper said in unison, things slipping into place.

"That makes things interesting, doesn't it?" Jared said.

TWENTY-TWO

"I'm not sure this is a good idea," Harper said, increasing her pace as she followed a furious Linden and Josh down the corridor toward the family's personal living space. "I think we should come up with a plan first."

"This is the plan, Heart," Jared said, gathering her hand and tugging her until she was close enough for him to wrap his arm around her waist. "We're going to ask Trask why he didn't mention his brother was the head of the murder mystery troupe."

"What good is that going to do?"

"I want to know," Linden said, stopping in front of the door and digging in his pocket for his key. "This whole thing is a mess and I don't understand what's going on."

"Even if Hal is Trask's brother – and I suggest we find Hal to confirm that first – that doesn't necessarily mean Trask has anything to do with his brother's death," Harper pointed out. "It could be something else entirely."

"Why are you fighting this?" Jared asked, confused. "You hated Trask from the moment you saw him."

"So did you," Harper pointed out. "He's a jackass. I'm not saying he's a great guy. Something about this feels wrong to me, though. I think we should call Mel and see what he can find on Trask before we do this."

"No way," Linden said. "This is my home and this is my hotel. I want answers."

"But ... ."

"No," Linden said, firmly shaking his head. "I need to know what's going on under my own roof. I lived in a cloud for years. I made terrible decisions and this family – my son especially – suffered. I can't fix everything, but I can move forward."

"That's admirable," Jared said. "We're behind you."

"I'm not," Harper grumbled, making a face when Jared glanced in her direction. "Something is going to go wrong. I know it."

"It's four against one, Heart," Jared said. "I think we'll be able to handle a sixty-five-year-old man."

Harper wasn't convinced Jared was correct, but she followed him into the Stokes' suite anyway, gasping when she saw the ornate room and over-the-top decorations that assailed her eyes upon entry. "Wow," she intoned, her blue eyes busy as they scanned the room. "Liberace just called and he wants his candelabra back."

Josh snickered. "My mother has unique taste," he said. "That ballroom was only the tip of the iceberg."

"I can't wait to meet her," Harper said.

"You won't be saying that five minutes from now," Josh said, his eyes thoughtful as they washed over Harper.

"What?" Harper asked, suddenly feeling uncomfortable.

"It's nothing," Josh said. "My father thinks you remind him of my mother. I guess I was trying to see ... something."

"You and your father are going to have a lot of time to talk about your mother," Harper said. "You're not going to get all of the information – or answers, for that matter – that you want in one sitting. It's going to take time.

"If you're lucky, though, you're going to be able to get to know a whole other set of family members," she continued. "Your mother probably still has family out there, and they're going to have photos and stories. You'll get to know her through them. It won't be the same, but it will still be something."

"And you're going to help her move on, right?" Josh pressed. "You said there was a better place out there for her."

"A lot of ghosts move on themselves when someone solves their murder ... or whatever secret they were hanging onto is revealed," Harper said. "If Alice can't move on herself, though, Zander and I can help her. We've done it before."

"Well, I almost hope she needs help," Josh said. "I'm dying to meet the famous Zander."

"You can do that regardless," Jared interjected. "You can visit Whisper Cove whenever you want. To get the full Zander and Harper effect it almost helps to sit through a meal with them in their home. They're not ever on their best behavior then."

Josh chuckled. "I don't want to miss that."

"You definitely don't," Jared agreed.

The trio followed Linden into the sitting room, pulling up short when they noticed the agitated woman sitting on the settee. Her dark hair was pulled back into a severe bun and her turtleneck looked tight enough to choke the life out of her. If her expression was to be believed, Harper was convinced it had already choked the fun out of her.

"That's Janet," Jared whispered to Harper.

"I kind of figured that out on my own," Harper said.

"What is going on?" Janet asked, getting to her feet. "Is there a reason I'm being bothered by these ... people ... in my own home?"

"Janet, this is Jared Monroe," Linden said, tugging on his limited patience as he fought to remain calm. "He was Josh's roommate in college. I'm sure you remember him."

"Do I get a prize if I do?" Janet challenged.

Linden frowned. "This is his girlfriend Harper Harlow," he added. "She's from Whisper Cove."

"That's even less exciting than the news that Josh's college room-mate is here," Janet deadpanned. "What do you want? I ask for very little under my own roof – especially since it's not really my roof now that you've opened it to vagabonds – but I do ask that you not invade my personal space for anything less than dire circumstances."

"These are dire circumstances," Linden said. "Have you seen Trask?"

Janet knit her eyebrows together. "I guess I saw him about two hours ago. Why do you ask?"

"We need to speak to him," Linden answered. "It seems his brother was part of the mystery troupe and he's gone missing. I'm sure that you remember we banished Hal from the property years ago when he tried to steal that ring of yours."

"Oh, of course," Janet said, leaning forward as intrigue finally dislodged the stick Harper was convinced was living in a very uncomfortable place amongst her posterior. "Wait, so you're saying that Hal was part of the mystery troupe I told you not to invite here? I'm shocked."

Harper made a face. She expected to dislike Janet, but the woman didn't have to make it so easy.

"We need to talk to Trask, Janet," Josh said, his voice chilly as he looked over the woman he called "mother" only an hour before.

Janet furrowed her brow as she shifted her attention to Josh. "Since when do you call me by my first name?"

"Since now," Josh answered.

"Is this because I wouldn't let you use the ballroom for your stupid event?" Janet challenged. "I don't care how petulant you get, I'm not allowing those people in that room. They'll ruin it. That room is a showplace and I want it to be exactly how it is when we reclaim this house."

"You're never going to reclaim this house, Janet," Josh snapped. "The house is gone. This is a hotel now. We're not going to somehow get all of the lost money back. We put a ton of money in renovations. This is a hotel now. It's never going to be just a house again."

"Stop calling me by my first name," Janet ordered. "That is not how things are done in polite society. I am your mother. You will treat me with respect."

"You're not my mother." The words were out of Josh's mouth before he had a chance to think better of them.

Harper's eyes widened as she risked a glance in Jared's direction, but he was impassive. Linden sighed at Josh's admission, but he didn't otherwise appear upset.

"I *am* your mother," Janet said. "You might not like it, but you're going to have to get over that."

"You're not my mother," Josh repeated. "Dad told me the truth tonight."

"And what truth is that?" Janet asked, feigning ignorance.

"He knows about Alice," Linden said. "That's why he called me down there. He had questions."

"We agreed that he was never to know about Alice," Janet said. "I am his mother. I raised him."

"Alice Thorpe gave birth to him, though," Harper said. "She's the one who loved him."

"I don't believe anyone was talking to you," Janet hissed. "Stay out of our private family affairs. In fact, get out of my home. I don't want you here."

"Leave her alone," Josh said. "They're with me. They can be here as long as I say they can be here."

"Maybe you're not invited to stay here any longer either," Janet suggested. "If I'm not your mother, that means you're not my son."

Harper was horrified by the way Janet talked to Josh. For his part, Josh seemed unmoved, almost relieved even. Finding out Janet wasn't his mother wasn't quite the blow Harper envisioned.

"Harper and Jared found out about Alice and they asked Josh because they were confused," Linden supplied, fudging the discovery details slightly. "When Josh asked, I decided to tell him the truth. He deserves it."

"What about what I deserve, Linden?" Janet asked. "Am I ever going to get what I deserve?"

"If you're lucky, a house will fly by the window before this storm lets up and land right on you," Harper suggested. "I'm pretty sure you deserve that."

Josh and Jared snickered despite the surreal nature of the situation and even Linden looked amused. Janet was another story.

"I can see you're pretty pleased with yourself," Janet said. "I have no idea why, though. You told Josh a secret he didn't need to know and now you're giving me a headache. You might consider that a win on the day, but to me it's merely tedious."

"We didn't come up here for this," Linden said. "We need to find Trask. Are you sure you don't know where he is?"

"I have no idea where Trask is," Janet said, rolling her eyes as she turned back to the settee. "I'm not his keeper and he's not mine. Now get out of my home."

Linden turned to leave, but Harper wasn't quite ready to let Janet off the hook yet.

"Did you kill Alice because you wanted her life?" Harper asked.

"Harper," Jared warned, widening his eyes as he glanced around the room. "You can't just ask questions like that."

"I'm actually curious to hear the answer, too," Josh interjected.

"Alice died of a heart attack in her sleep," Janet said. "I didn't cause that. I don't care how evil you think I am. I don't have magical powers."

Janet's blithe dismissal of the charge wasn't enough to dissuade Harper. "Alice Thorpe was drugged and then smothered in her sleep," she challenged. "Whoever did it had to have a motive. Josh was obviously too young and Linden was in love with her. That leaves you."

Linden balked. "You can't possibly think Janet killed her best friend."

"I honestly don't know," Harper admitted. "I'm not sure that there's another explanation, though. If it wasn't Janet, who was it?"

"But … ." Linden broke off, working his jaw up and down as he racked his memory. When he finally let his eyes fall on Janet, he looked conflicted. "You didn't kill Alice, did you?"

"How can you possibly ask me that?" Janet snapped. "I was the one who took care of your son when Alice died because you were too drunk and depressed to get out of bed. I took care of both of you. How dare you accuse me of anything like that."

"That wasn't a denial," Jared said, taking a step closer so he was at an even level with Josh and Linden and leaving Harper in a protected position behind him. "Did you kill Alice? It would make sense in a way. You were jealous of her and you always had a crush on Linden. Perhaps you chose to take the life you always wanted."

"That's the most ridiculous thing I've ever heard," Janet said. "I'm the hero in this story, people. I'm the one who kept this family together. I'm the one who made sure the Stokes name stayed great … well, until you guys managed to ruin it by opening a hotel, that is. Still, I'm the one who did everything for this family. I can't believe you would even consider accusing me of something like this."

"That's still not a denial," Jared said pointedly.

"God, Janet, did you kill my Alice?" Linden asked, tears filling his eyes. "Did you kill Alice with your bare hands in one room and then walk into the next room and pick up her son so you could steal him?"

Janet remained defiant. "You have no idea what you're talking about," she gritted out. "You're not smart enough to grasp the things I had to do to keep this family together."

"Well, I'm going to take you into custody and turn you over to the local police," Jared said. "You can explain to them what you've done and I'm going to trust that they're smart enough to figure out your motivations on their own."

"I'm not going with you," Janet scoffed. "You have no jurisdiction here and I haven't done anything wrong. You can't take me."

"Do you want to bet?" Jared challenged. "I am fully within my rights to take you into custody, and that's exactly what I plan on doing."

"I don't think so," Janet screeched. "You can't take me! I won't allow it!"

Harper was enjoying the show until she realized someone was behind her. It was too late to turn around – or alert Jared – and the cool tip of a knife pressing against her tender throat caused her heart to constrict. Trask grabbed her neck and slammed her back until her body was flush with his, making sure she had no wiggle room or avenue of escape.

"No one is taking Janet anywhere," Trask said. "Unless, of course, you want this one to die. I'm kind of curious which way the decision is going to go."

TWENTY-THREE

"Let her go!"

Jared took a step in Trask's direction and only eased up when Trask prodded Harper's neck with the knife, causing her to whimper.

"Don't tell me what to do, boy," Trask warned. "It's not going to end well for anyone if you get too big for your britches. Or, am I reading the situation wrong? Do you want me to kill her? If so, keep flapping your yap."

Jared's face contorted. "Give her to me." He extended his hand. "She hasn't done anything to you. I ... please give her to me."

"Trask, you unhand that woman right now," Linden barked. He was flustered but refused to let the situation get away from him. "That's an order."

Trask forced out an eerie laugh. It was more malevolent than amused. "An order? Do you honestly think you're in a position to give me orders?" Trask jerked his hand and jabbed the point of the knife into Harper's throat. It was hard enough to draw blood – and elicit a muted sob – but nothing else.

"Jared," Harper said, her voice low. "Maybe you should listen to what he has to say."

Jared met Harper's terrified gaze. "It's going to be okay," he said. "I'm right here. I'm … so sorry. I should've paid better attention."

"It's fine," Harper said, tugging on her limited courage to bolster both Jared and herself. "This isn't your fault. You need to know that in case … ."

"Don't finish that sentence," Jared warned. "You'll be here with me very soon. I promised you a game of hopping soap tonight, and you know I always keep my promises."

"Except when you say you'll call." Harper was going for levity, but it fell flat.

"Heart … ." Jared had no idea what to say.

"What do you want, Trask?" Josh asked, his heart going out to Jared. He'd never seen his friend look so helpless, and while Harper was strong and refused to fall apart, Josh could tell she was terrified. "I don't understand what you think you're doing. How do you think this is going to end?"

"How do you think this is going to end?" Trask challenged, tightening his grip on Harper's throat. "Do you think you're going to talk me out of this? No matter what you think is going to happen, I can promise you're way off."

"Don't you even think about hurting her," Jared hissed, his eyes flashing. "Let go of her throat."

"Take a step back, Detective Monroe," Trask said, his voice cold and detached.

"No," Jared said, shaking his head. "I don't trust you."

Trask squeezed Harper's throat again, causing her to gasp.

"Dammit, Trask! Leave her alone," Linden snapped. "What are you thinking? I don't understand why you're doing this."

"Of course you don't," Trask said. "You don't understand anything. That's why you married Alice in the first place. I thought you were finally going to toe the line and do what you were supposed to do for this family when you married Janet … but that didn't happen, did it?"

Linden was dumbfounded. "What are you talking about?"

"God, you're so stupid," Trask spat. "Even now you're lost. Why am I not surprised?"

HARPER FOCUSED ON REGULATING HER OXYGEN INTAKE SO SHE didn't pass out. *Breathe in. Breathe out.* Her mind didn't seem to be firing on all cylinders. She tried to wrap her head around Trask's appearance – and what it meant in the grand scheme of things – but all she could think about was the knife.

She lifted her eyes and locked gazes with Jared. He looked petrified. She wanted to touch him. She wanted to tell him everything was going to be okay. She didn't think she could make that promise, though. She knew something was wrong when they entered the family suite, and for some reason she ignored her inner danger alarm. She had no one to blame but herself.

Alice appeared at her side, causing Harper to jolt.

"This doesn't look good," Alice said.

"What was your first clue?" Harper muttered.

"Did you say something?" Trask asked, jerking at Harper's throat. "Are you mouthing off?"

"I was just … talking to myself," Harper replied, forcing herself to remain calm even though she really wanted to panic.

Understanding flitted across Jared's face as he shot Harper a reassuring smile. "She talks to herself all the time," he said. "It helps her calm down."

"So you're saying she's crazy?" Trask challenged. "That doesn't surprise me. I knew something was off about her from the moment I saw her."

"That's because she's low class," Janet said.

"Probably," Trask agreed.

Harper made a face but otherwise remained still. She shifted her eyes to Alice, who watched Trask with an unreadable face.

"What's the plan here, Trask?" Jared asked. "Why did you even get involved in this?"

"I have to protect the mistress of the house," Trask replied. "That's my job."

Harper wet her lips, an idea forming. "You killed Alice, didn't you?"

Alice nodded. "He did." Her voice was barely a whisper. "He's the one who snuck into my room that night. He wasn't alone, though."

"Alice was a problem," Trask intoned, his voice taking on a theatrical quality. "She was a nice girl who didn't understand her station. This was a grand house with a grand lineage. You let it fall by the wayside, Linden. I tried to tell you back then, but you wouldn't listen."

"What is he talking about?" Josh asked, confused.

"When I decided to marry your mother I talked to my father first," Linden answered, searching his memory. "He was pleased with my decision, but my mother was ... less than thrilled. She thought Alice was nice but not ready to take on the importance of the Stokes' family name.

"Harsens Island is small and the Stokes family was considered royalty on a very tiny island," he continued. "That never mattered to me and it didn't matter to my father. It mattered to my mother a great deal and she fought my engagement to Alice.

"My father talked to Alice's father and they both agreed to the marriage right away," Linden said. "I proposed with my father's blessing and I thought that was the end of it. My mother put in a pouty appearance at the wedding and then went back to her life of ... teas and whatever else she did.

"Four years after the wedding my mother took ill and died," Linden said. "Up until that point, Alice and I were allowed to do whatever we wanted and were left out of most of the social gatherings that went on here. That all changed after my mother died."

"How so?" Josh asked.

"Alice had to take on the role of social matriarch and it didn't fit her well," Linden explained. "Alice was happiest in her garden. We were planning a family, although she didn't get pregnant as early as we hoped. Still, when my father asked her to take on the duties, she did it without complaint.

"Unfortunately she didn't do it to everyone's liking," Linden said, inclining his chin in Trask's direction. "She switched over my mother's stuffy garden parties to charity events. She didn't see the point of holding Daughters of the American Revolution parties because she thought they were antiquated. Alice wanted to bring the Stokes family into the present day, and Trask didn't like that."

"Alice was beneath this family," Trask said. "We all knew it. Romance is fine when you're young and dumb, but you had responsibilities, Linden, and picking a suitable mate was one of them."

"I married for love," Linden said. "The only one who thought this family was supposed to be special was you. My father didn't believe that. He loved Alice."

"Your father didn't see the big picture, just like you and Josh don't see the big picture," Trask seethed. "The only one who sees the big picture is Janet. She always has. She was meant for the position she holds. You just didn't see it."

"You drugged Alice's drink at dinner and then snuck into her room and smothered her when she was out," Harper said. "She was too drugged to fight back, and no one bothered to do a thorough autopsy. I'm guessing it had something to do with the Stokes' family station."

"You have no proof of that," Trask argued.

"You weren't alone," Harper said, locking gazes with Jared. "You had Janet with you that night. Alice made a mistake when she became friends with Janet. She didn't realize how big of a mistake it was until it was too late."

"That's ridiculous," Janet scoffed, although she looked mildly alarmed. "How can you even spout nonsense like that?"

"You glommed on to Alice in high school because she was dating Linden," Harper said, working through the clues as she talked. "You wanted to be close to Linden because you always had dreams of living in the big house. You wanted to figure out a way to make Linden fall for you.

"The problem was that you didn't have much of a personality, did you?" she continued. "You weren't fun like Alice. You weren't beautiful like Alice either. No matter how hard you tried, you couldn't make Linden notice you. Even worse, when you weren't around Linden and Alice made jokes about your crush on him behind your back."

"That's a lie!" Janet exploded.

Harper ignored the outburst. "When you found out Alice and Linden were going to be married you panicked," she said. "You knew you had to do something. I'm betting you approached Linden's mother and explained why Alice wasn't a suitable mate. Am I right?"

"Alice wasn't a suitable mate," Janet shot back. "I didn't do anything untoward. I was honest. I told Alice she didn't belong in this house. She laughed it off as if it was a joke. She didn't deserve to be a part of this family. She refused to listen to me."

"At some point you realized Trask was the best ally you had in this house," Harper said. "You approached him with a plan and he gladly accepted it. When was that? Was it before or after Alice realized she was pregnant with Josh?"

"It was before actually," Janet said, refusing to stand on pretense. "I still wanted to kill her so I could provide the Stokes' heir, but Trask refused. He said we had to wait until Alice gave birth in case Linden never moved on and had another child. We had to be sure the Stokes' line was safe.

"I hated Trask for insinuating that Linden and I would never have a child at the time, but it looks like he was right," she continued. "I got everything I thought I wanted after Alice died and none of it meant a thing."

"That's because Linden didn't love you," Harper said, risking a glance at Alice. She looked angry. "Alice was the love of Linden's life and he never got over her. He eventually agreed to marry you because he needed help with Josh and you seemed eager to take over the house – something he couldn't be bothered with.

"You thought you were going to convince him to fall in love with you eventually," she continued. "You thought he would see you with Josh and realize he'd overlooked you, maybe even forget all about Alice. That never happened, though, and it made you mean and bitter.

"Still, you managed to put up with things because you didn't have any other options," Harper said. "You were the master of your domain, after all. It just wasn't the life you envisioned. Josh grew up to be the apple of his father's eye and you hated him because you couldn't provide an heir to cement your position in the family. Was that because you were incapable, or did Linden refuse to touch you?"

It was a calculated gamble, but Harper was tired of waiting for something to happen. She was ready to force the issue.

"Wait a second," Josh said, realization dawning. "Are you saying ... oh, wow."

"What are you saying?" Alice asked, confused.

"I'm saying that Linden and Janet never consummated their relationship," Harper said, knowing she should rein in her smugness and failing. "She couldn't provide an heir if Linden wasn't up for the challenge, so to speak."

"Holy crap," Jared said. "That's probably why she's so bitter."

"I know I would be that bitter if I had to go so long without … comfort," Harper said.

"What does that have to do with anything?" Janet was shrill. "You're not supposed to talk about things like that in public."

"What does it matter now?" Linden challenged. "Everyone is going to find out what you did. You killed my wife. You killed her! You and Trask worked together to … ruin … this family. I hope you're happy."

"Why would I be happy?" Janet spat. "You turned my life into a living hell. All I had was the money and then you took that away. Why would I possibly be happy?"

"You got everything you ever wanted, though," Harper said. "You got the house and the husband. You just didn't get the love. That didn't play into your game, and you still don't understand how a real marriage works. It's almost sad."

"What about Hal?" Josh asked. "How does he fit into this?"

"I'm guessing that Trask made sure Hal's group was the one hired for this event because it was supposed to go wrong," Harper supplied. "Trask said the event was beneath the family and he obviously wanted it to fail. Unfortunately for him, his brother was a deadbeat and lowlife and he didn't like to play by the rules."

"Hal actually demanded more money," Trask said. "He was supposed to make sure everyone had a rotten time. I thought the storm would only add to that. Instead everyone had the audacity to enjoy themselves. I knew that would encourage Josh to try more of this … nonsense.

"This is a home, not a hotel," he continued. "It was never meant for the masses. It was meant for the privileged few. I confronted Hal and told him he had to do something to rock the boat and he demanded more money. It was money I didn't have ready access to in the storm. He threatened to go to Linden so … he had to go."

"Where is his body?" Jared asked.

"I have no idea," Trask replied. "I seem to have forgotten where it is. You can't convict without a body. I saw it on television."

Harper glanced at Alice for confirmation.

"He's lying," Alice said. "I found a body in the wine cellar. He wrapped it in a tarp and put it behind the casks in the far corner."

"Hal's body is behind some wine barrels in the basement," Harper announced.

Trask tightened his grip on her throat. "How do you know that?"

Harper's face reddened as she gasped for breath.

"Get your hands off of her!" Jared bellowed. "Don't touch her!"

Trask ground the tip of the knife into Harper's neck in a circular motion. "Don't tell me what to do! I'm in charge here."

Harper briefly pressed her eyes shut so she could gain control of her panic and when she flipped her lids open again she saw Jared watching her. For some reason she was more worried about him – how he would react should something happen to her – rather than her own plight. It was a sobering thought.

"What do you want, Trask?" Jared asked, his voice cracking. "There's no way out of this. Too many people know what you've done. Are you going to kill all of us?"

"I am," Trask confirmed.

Jared stilled. "And how do you think you're going to get away with that?"

"I have the solution in the basement," Trask answered. "I'm going to kill you and blame it on my missing brother. He was jealous of the Stokes family, you see. He always has been. They banned him from the property years ago because he was a thief.

"That will leave Janet and I to save the family legacy," he continued. "We'll build the Stokes family back to what it should've been all along. Of course we won't have an heir, but we can always adopt a ward down the line."

"There's no money, you idiot," Josh snapped. "We're not hiding money from you. Where do you think you're going to find money to run this place?"

"I'm sure something fortuitous will happen," Trask replied blandly.

"They already have money socked away," Harper interjected, the rest of the puzzle slipping into place. "They've been hoarding money for years. That's why Janet was so upset when you put her on an allowance and sold most of her things.

"It wasn't that she didn't want to give back her purchases – although I'm sure that chafed – but she really didn't want to lose access to the money she's been putting aside for herself," she continued. "Janet is a survivor, and once she realized she was never going to convince Linden to fall in love with her, she had to come up with a backup plan.

"Think about it," Harper prodded. "In the back of her head Janet always knew there was a chance Linden would come to his senses and give her the boot. She had no real standing in this house or family without an heir."

"That does make sense," Josh mused. "When I looked at the books I couldn't believe how much money she burned through over the years."

"That's because she didn't burn through it all," Jared said. "Still, you could've left after the financial collapse and no one would've been the wiser, Janet. Why stay?"

"The house," Harper answered. "She's always been infatuated with the house."

"It's my house," Janet said. "It's going to stay my house. We'll blame your murders on Hal, I'll go through a very public mourning period, and then we'll right this sinking ship."

"It's a great plan," Harper said.

"I know."

"There's only one problem," Harper said. "We've been in touch with a Whisper Cove police detective and one of my business associates and they're aware of what's going on out here. They know Hal is dead so you can't use him as a scapegoat."

Trask stilled, surprised. "How?"

"I told them."

"How do you know?"

Harper smiled at Alice. It seemed her big secret was about to be everyone's saving grace. "Because I can see and talk to ghosts."

"What?" Trask was flabbergasted. "That's not a thing. No one believes that."

"Everyone in Whisper Cove believes that," Jared challenged. "You don't have a play here."

"That doesn't mean I'm going to let her go," Trask snapped, grabbing Harper's hair and giving it a vicious yank as he turned her. "I want to see you when I kill you."

Jared moved quickly. He knew he was out of time. He grabbed the knife before Trask could slash it against Harper's throat. Jared didn't have a good angle, but he put up one heck of a fight as he worked to protect his blonde.

Harper took advantage of the situation and slammed her knee in Trask's groin, taking him by surprise. When he didn't relinquish the knife she sank her teeth into the soft flesh next to his wrist, causing him to yowl in pain.

He dropped the knife and it clattered to the floor. Harper kicked it away with her free foot while Jared slammed his fist into Trask's face, causing the older man to buckle to his knees.

"Don't ever touch her again!" Jared yelled, pounding his fist into Trask's face a second time. "I will kill you if you ever try and touch her again!"

"I think he gets it, man," Josh said, appearing at Jared's side and placing a hand on his shoulder to stop him from hitting Trask a third time. "He won't touch her again. I promise."

Jared regained his senses and turned to find Harper watching him. He took two steps and grabbed her, dragging her into his arms as he buried his face in her flaxen hair. "I thought I was going to lose you there for a second."

"That can never happen," Harper said, returning the embrace. "I don't like to lose and we haven't solved the case of the hopping soap yet."

Jared weakly chuckled, although the laughter shifted to a sob as he tightened his arms around Harper's back. "Don't scare me like that again."

"Ugh, I think I'm going to throw up," Janet said, rolling her eyes from her spot next to Linden. She didn't make a move to flee or fight. She seemed resigned.

"Just for the record, I would like to point out I had a bad feeling when we walked into this room," Harper said. "I told you and no one listened to me."

Jared leaned back his head, incredulous. "Really? You're going to bring that up now?"

"I told you I like to win."

"I'm going to … hug the crap out of you and then kill you," Jared said, pulling her back against his chest. "You're going to be the death of me, Heart."

"But what a way to go," Josh teased.

TWENTY-FOUR

J ared woke to the sound of chirping birds the next morning, shifting his eyes to the window and smiling when he saw the sun peeking through. It had been so long since he saw it, he almost forgot what it looked like. Then memories of Harper's ordeal flooded his mind and he turned, worried he would discover her side of the bed empty. Instead he found her Skyping with Zander.

"I can't believe you solved a case without me," Zander said, his pout pronounced. He was in bed, too. "I feel so neglected, Harp. When are you coming home?"

"I don't know," Harper answered. "We have to talk to the police again today and fill out reports. I'm sorry you feel neglected, but we'll be home as soon as we can. It just might not be today. I'm sorry."

"That sucks," Zander muttered.

"We're coming home today," Jared announced, rolling so he was next to Harper and rested his head against her shoulder. He smiled at Zander. "I wouldn't dream of keeping you two apart for another night."

"Are you sure?" Harper asked, relief and hope washing over her. "What about the police?"

"We told them most of what we knew last night," Jared replied, leaning up so he could kiss Harper's cheek. She was soft and warm, which told him she hadn't been awake for very long. "If they have more questions, they know where to find us."

"Did Janet and Trask admit what they did?" Zander asked.

"Janet did," Jared replied. "She doesn't seem to think she did anything wrong, which is dumbfounding. Trask, however, is obviously going for an insanity defense. He claims we're making up everything and he has no idea what we're talking about."

"Did they find Hal's body?"

"It was in the basement," Harper said. "Alice showed me and I showed the police."

"What about Alice?" Zander asked. "Is she going on her own, or does she need our help?"

"She's asked for some time to watch Linden and Josh adjust to their new life," Harper answered. "I have a feeling she's going to let go on her own, but if she's still here in six months she wants us to help her move on."

"And Hal?"

"He's gone as far as I can tell," Harper said. "I never saw him again. He might've let go before we found his body. The body also might've been a catalyst for him to stay. I just don't know."

"He was a douche anyway," Zander said. "Maybe he's off hanging out with Archibald."

Harper giggled, the sound warming Jared's heart. "They would be quite the pair," she said.

"What does that mean for Linden and Josh?" Zander asked. "Are they going to keep the hotel open?"

"They're going to have some financial options once they find out where Janet stashed her money, but neither one of them want to go back to the life they were living before the financial crisis," Jared answered. "I think they're going to leave the hotel open, and even implement some of Harper's ideas. They've even made noise about hiring you guys to run haunted tours in the fall."

"They have?" Harper was surprised.

"They have," Jared confirmed. "I think it's just a way for Josh to hit on you some more, but who am I to argue when my girlfriend and one of my best friends have success on the brain?"

"You don't have to worry about him flirting," Harper said. "I'm pretty happy with my current boyfriend."

"That's good," Jared whispered. "He's pretty happy with you, too."

"Ugh. Don't make me throw up," Zander said. "If you do it in front of me I'm going to throw up."

"You're such a joy sometimes," Jared deadpanned.

"I'm anxious for you guys to come home," Zander said. "Not only do I miss you, Harp, but I find I miss Jared, too. It's very upsetting."

"Why is that upsetting?" Jared asked.

"You stole my Harper and now you're stealing my heart," Zander teased. "I don't know why it's upsetting. It just is. I was lonely this week. I think that means I need to get a boyfriend."

"I miss you, too," Harper said, grinning. "We'll be home this afternoon. If you're good, maybe we can beg Jared to grill steaks. We never did get our surf and turf last night."

"I forgot about that," Jared said. "Maybe we can convince Josh to supply us with steaks and lobster tails before we go? I think that's the least he could do since we told him the truth about his mother ... and got him and his father away from Janet and Trask."

"That's a great idea," Harper enthused, grinning.

"Speaking of great ideas, we have exactly one hour before breakfast and I want to spend it in the bathtub," Jared said, reaching for the phone. "Say goodbye to Zander."

"Wait a second," Zander protested. "We've only been on the phone for five minutes. I need more time with Harper if you don't want me to go insane."

"And you'll have her for as long as you want very soon," Jared said. "I want to enjoy the last two hours of our vacation, and I can't do that if we have an audience."

"You're such a pig," Zander said, making a face. "I can't believe I missed you."

"That makes two of us," Jared said. "Say goodbye, Zander."

"Goodbye, Zander," Zander deadpanned, although his smile was impish. "I'll see you guys soon."

Jared disconnected the phone and tossed it on the other side of the bed as he rolled on top of Harper. "Now that it's just the two of us, we have to discuss how frightened I was last night," he said. "I think you're going to need to make me feel better before breakfast. Otherwise I might cry or something."

Harper laughed. "How good are we talking here?"

"Very good," Jared said, nuzzling his face against her cheek for a moment. "I was really scared, and now I want to be really happy." He was playing a game, but the words came from a place of total honesty. "I don't want to be that scared ever again."

"That makes two of us," Harper said, rubbing Jared's shoulders. "We're okay, though. Not only are we okay, but we have the world's biggest bathtub at our disposal ... and Josh sent up eight bars of soap before we went to sleep last night."

"I guess we'd better get on that," Jared said, kissing the tip of Harper's nose and climbing out of bed. "Let's finish our vacation in style, Heart. Then we can go home and be really happy."

"That sounds like the perfect way to spend a day to me."

77757209R00114

Made in the USA
Lexington, KY
03 January 2018